HER DIRTY DOCTORS

THE MEN AT WORK SERIES

MIKA LANE

HEADLANDS PUBLISHING

COPYRIGHT

BE THE FIRST TO KNOW...

Want more heat, heart,
and bad boys who know what they're doing?
Join my list and I'll send the steam straight to your inbox,
starting with a deliciously naughty story:

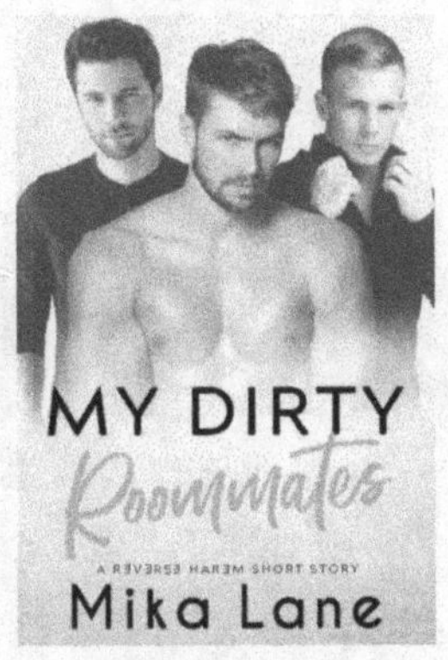

SIGN UP TO MY MAILING LIST!
Or visit:
https://geni.us/free-book-signup

CHARLEIGH "CHAR" BIDDLE

"**D**rop me here."

I threw a dirty look to my left. I meant business.

It worked.

He pulled up to the red curb, where regular folks were never to stop their cars, and pushed the gearshift of his sleek, black Mercedes into *park*.

I looked at my father, the man I'd once adored. The one who'd taught me to ride a bike and who'd picked me up and dusted me off after I'd wiped out so hard I had gravel stuck in my knee.

The same man who'd helped me with my math

homework and who held me when I cried because the girl down the street had been mean to me.

That man—that *father*—no longer existed.

He was completely and tragically gone.

The man I looked at now had cold, dead eyes, sallow skin, and two thin, straight lines for lips. The cords on his neck disappeared into a too-big dress shirt collar, which was unsuccessfully cinched up with a blue silk Zegna necktie.

Sometimes the best money can buy still looks like shit.

"Don't forget what we talked about. So help me, Char," he said, his tone menacing.

Even his voice was ugly. Hateful. Poisonous.

The pain of losing your dad to a person you no longer know? There are no words for it.

A screeching ambulance pulled up behind us, turning up the velocity of its siren to warn us to get the hell out of the way.

Yeah, we were parked where the ambulances pulled up to the emergency room. And my dad did not give a shit.

He was like that.

Instead of moving, he rolled down his car window, leaning out to unceremoniously scream at the ambulance driver. "Turn that goddamn thing off," he bellowed.

I whipped around in my seat, clutching the fluffy

white towel absorbing the blood flowing from the palm of my hand. The driver, when he realized who my dad was, flipped off the siren, which died with a sad, slow whine. Meanwhile, the EMTs jumped out of the vehicle to wheel their patient into the ER, muscling the gurney up and over the curb since Dad was blocking the ramp that would have made their job much easier.

Such. An. Asshole.

As the transport team rolled their patient through the doors, one of them turned around and hollered through the open passenger window, past me, to Dad.

"'Morning, Mr. Biddle. Good to see you."

I looked down to hide my face. I didn't want the guy, or anyone for that matter, to see me. My father was not a good person to be associated with.

Harsh, but true.

Dad started to open his driver's side door, but I quickly put a hand on his arm before he got out.

"You don't have to come in. I can take care of this."

I pulled my hand back. I didn't like touching him.

He looked at his watch. "Fine. Just as well. Your mother and I have that charity luncheon. We can't be late."

I hated that he called my stepmother, my *mother*. He should just call her Iris, like I did.

But I didn't bother reminding him Iris was not my mother. I'd been doing it for years and it didn't stop him.

He put the car in *drive* before I'd even opened my door, and looked over my way as if to say *you can leave now.*

In the minutes since we'd sat parked outside the ER, I'd been scanning the people coming and going. When I was confident no one would see me, I hopped out, cradling my bloody hand. Without so much as a good-bye, Dad pressed the gas. The car's forward momentum pulled my open door shut before I could do it myself, with the solid thud cars of that caliber have. Dad was hermetically sealed in his little fort of luxury he believed only people like him were entitled to.

I'd had a Prius until recently, when it went into the shop. It was taking a strangely long time for its ten-year-old engine to be serviced—something, I was quite sure, that had to do with my dad's instructions to the mechanic.

Dad accelerated with a screech and was out of sight before I'd even reached the doors of Headlands Hospital's ER. The hospital where my father was CEO. And served as general overlord.

"Hi," I said to the intake clerk.

Her head snapped up from her computer. It was clearly, and thankfully, a slow moment there. I was not down with being around a bunch of people right now, especially well-meaning ones who would ask me what had happened to my hand and how.

The clerk looked me up and down, trying to assess my reason for coming to the ER, convinced that since I was still standing on my own two feet, I couldn't be that bad off. I raised my hand for her to see, the white towel bundled around it now pretty much soaked red with blood.

"Oh my," she said, reaching under her desk. "Here, please put this around it." She handed me a plastic bag.

Smart.

I should have thought to take one of those before leaving the house, but in my adrenaline-fueled state, all I'd done was grab one of my stepmom's expensive Frette towels from the linen closet. Now encircled in a plastic baggie, my bloody mess was contained, but the towel was a lost cause. I'd have to find somewhere to chuck it before I went back home. Would Iris notice it missing? In the past, I'd ask a maid to take care of a problem like this and no one would know any better. But my dad and stepmom didn't have a maid anymore. For that matter, they didn't have any household help any longer.

"Here's my ID and insurance card."

The clerk took them from me, and as she entered my name in the computer, did a double take. I knew what she was thinking. And I knew what she wanted to ask.

Is your dad...?

But she didn't. Thank god.

"Okay. Charleigh Biddle," she said to herself, banging loudly on her keyboard.

Finally looking up at me, she asked, "What did you do to yourself?"

"Cut myself slicing a bagel." I shrugged, pretending to be embarrassed over such a silly kitchen accident.

She nodded knowingly and continued typing into the computer. "Okay. We see a lot of those. Go have a seat, Charleigh. Someone will be with you shortly."

I grabbed a hard, plastic chair in the ER's clean but utilitarian waiting room. There was a tattered copy of *Soccer World* on the seat next to me, the only reading material in sight, and a wall-mounted TV, which was thankfully turned off. A scruffy old man in the corner dozed in the otherwise empty room.

Dad had dropped me off at the ER at just the right time. When I glanced back at the clerk, there were already three people waiting in line and a family of four just arriving.

I scrolled through my phone with my good hand, relieved the clerk had either not realized or just not mentioned I was her boss's boss's boss's boss's daughter—or however many layers of management there were between her and the hospital's executive office. Biddle wasn't the most common name, but I'd often passed it off as pure coincidence that I shared the same surname as the head of the hospital. And I planned to continue to.

Since I'd started nursing school, I'd spent time in several different hospitals, rotating through every medical specialty as part of my training. Not surprisingly, none had ER waiting rooms quite as drab as the one I was sitting in right now. My father was a notoriously cheap CEO, unwilling to spend a dime more than he had to in order to make patients comfortable.

Another reason to distance myself from him. As if there weren't already enough.

2

CHAR

"Biddle? Charlene?" a nurse called.

I had one of *those* names.

"It's actually Charleigh," I said, pronouncing it like *Sharley*. I didn't bother explaining my nickname. I wouldn't be with her long enough.

"Gotcha. Sorry 'bout that. It's pretty, though, your name," she said, smiling as she pulled the privacy curtain closed on the treatment room she'd brought me to.

I appreciated her smile. I needed to remember how good they made people feel. Small things like that would come in handy when I started my own nursing job.

With a fucked-up hand.

I knew very well that just because I'd been ushered into a treatment room, it didn't mean I'd be seen by anyone right away. So, I settled into the chair next to the exam table and propped my injured hand on it, the first real chance I'd had to elevate it. Iris's towel was now ruined beyond hope.

I felt a tinge of petty satisfaction in that.

"Hello," a deep voice said.

I looked up.

Where was I?

In a hospital, or on an episode of some medical show where all the doctors were impossibly beautiful and always cured the sick people?

"I'm Dr. Bowie Grier."

Well.

He pushed a mop of curly dark hair behind each of his ears and smiled. His eyes crinkled, indicating he was old enough to be a real doctor and not a medical resident, his facial scruff signifying he was a cool, casual guy.

He was one of the most beautiful men I'd ever seen.

But my hand throbbed, reminding me I was not in a TV show with hot doctors, but rather a real ER where I needed to get the big cut in my palm fixed up before it bled all over the floor.

The doctor extended his hand to shake, glancing between me and a portable computer screen. After I gulped, I extended mine back. My good one.

Doctor Bowie Grier. He looked so familiar.

But why?

"What's going on for you today, Miss..." he consulted a portable computer screen, "Biddle?"

His expression changed when he said Biddle. As I'd known it would. Time for another lie. He looked back up at me, this time intently, and he tilted his head like he was trying to remember something.

Hope he hadn't forgotten the basics of suturing a cut.

"I was slicing a bagel," I said quickly, shrugging once again like it was no big deal—even though my hand was starting to hurt like a bitch.

"Ouch," he said, walking over to a sink to wash his hands.

He pushed a wheeled stool in my direction, and when he was right in front of me, took a seat. He stared at me for a moment. Did I look familiar to him, too?

"Mind if I have a look?" he asked with a slight smile.

"Please do."

He pulled on plastic gloves, then pulled the plastic bag off my hand, followed by the towel. Both items fell into the trashcan.

That had been a fifty-dollar hand towel.

Ask me if I cared.

"Hey," he said, turning my hand over and pressing on the palm to assess the bleeding, "are you any relation to Charles Biddle, the hospital CEO?"

I shook my head. "Nope. I'm not. Biddle's a common last name."

Yeah, right.

He knit his brow, studying me. Then he reached for a gauze pad and put pressure on the inch-long gash on my palm to stop the last of the leaking blood.

His touch sent through me a tremor of something I couldn't initially describe, even though my hand was hurting like hell. A second later I recognized it as a sensation of comfort and safety, two things I hadn't experienced in far too long.

Women must fall in love with this guy every freaking day.

He nodded, still poking around at my hand. "It doesn't really look too bad. You did a good job putting pressure on it before you got to me. But it's going to need stitches. You okay with that?"

He was so close to my hand while dabbing the blood off it that I could smell his hair. His clean, fresh hair.

And when the top of his scrubs fell open a bit, I saw the beginning of some seriously carved pecs.

Naturally, it turned out I wasn't the only one who found this man infinitely attractive. As the numbing shots he gave me took effect, the treatment room's curtain flew open.

"Dr. Grier," a woman in scrubs cooed, rushing in to join us. I couldn't read the name on her ID badge other than to see the word *nurse* in large, capital letters. I'd be wearing one of those soon.

"Can I do anything to help?" She pulled her shoulders back, pushed out her chest, and batted her fake eyelashes.

"Sure, thanks. You can help with these sutures," he said, pulling a curved needle attached to a thread out of a sterile packet.

He pinched together the skin on either side of my cut and slid the needle through, looking up at me quickly. "You might not want to watch."

No way was I telling him I was a nurse. "I'm good. Don't worry."

He looked up at his helper, who snipped the first stitch. "She's a tough one, huh?"

She glanced at me without a bit of interest and turned back to him. "Oh Dr. Grier, we're having birthday cake later today for—"

But he cut her off. "Char, how did you manage a deep cut right in the palm of your hand?"

He'd said my name correctly. No one ever said my name correctly on the first, or even subsequent tries.

The nurse must have clued him in. I'd have to remember that trick. It was a nice touch. *Say the patient's name right...*

But the nurse who'd just barged in didn't practice the same sort of pleasantries. She scowled at being cut off.

In between the stitches, he looked up at me again,

his eyes smiling. Shit, I would have cut off a finger if it meant I could spend more time with him.

I couldn't deny it. A favorite topic of conversation among nursing students involved rating the hot doctors.

Okay, that was messed up. Down girl.

"Char? Did you hear me? I asked how you cut yourself."

Why was he asking again? I'd already told him.

"Like I said, I was slicing a bagel."

Did he not believe me?

He nodded, but his expression indicated I was full of shit. "Hey, nurse, I think we're all good here," he said to Boobs and Eyelashes.

It took a moment for her to realize she was being dismissed. When she did, the scowl returned to her otherwise pleasant face. "Oh. Well. Okay."

She split.

I had no doubt he had nurses throwing themselves at him all the time. Doctors were fortunate in that regard, I'd been told.

But I'd also heard most of them were impressed-with-themselves douchebags.

He was bandaging my hand when he gave me a funny look. "Char, this… is not the type of injury you'd see from slicing a bagel. Normally your fingers would be cut. There wouldn't be a big wound in the palm of your hand."

He clearly expected me to change my story.

Which was not going to happen.

"Well, I must be extra clumsy then. Just pushed the knife right into my palm."

"Okay then," he said, handing me a small cup of water. "Next time wear a baseball mitt, okay?" He laughed.

"Absolutely. I am just so clumsy. Geez," I said, slapping my thigh.

He hesitated. "You can have your stitches removed by anyone, but if you want to come back here, I can help you out."

Well then. You can bet I'll be coming back. Even though I could take out my own stitches.

"Thanks, Dr. Grier."

But he didn't leave. "Char, you don't remember me, do you?"

I was right, he *did* look familiar.

"Oh wow, I was just thinking I knew you. Where'd you go to college?"

Stupid question. He was probably at least eight years older than me.

"Did you happen to take a ski trip to Aspen last year?"

I gulped, as the blood ran out of my face.

Oh god. Was he who I thought he was?

No. Impossible. What were the chances.

"Did you happen to hang out in the Ajax bar your last night in town?"

No, no, no. Please no.

"Um… I might have," I mumbled in a small voice.

I eyed the curtain behind him. I could make a run for it. Just dash out the door to wait for my BFF Alice to come pick me up.

The BFF who also happened to have been in Aspen with me.

He crossed his arms, leaning back against the treatment table, the movement pulling the sleeves of his scrub shirt tight around his rocky biceps.

Oh my god.

He nodded his head slowly.

"Um… did we…?"

I couldn't finish the sentence.

He just stared at me. Was he enjoying this?

Because I sure as hell was not.

"Yes, Char, we did."

3

CHAR

"How'd you get here so fast?" I asked, diving into Alice's Toyota pickup and sinking as low in my seat as I could. I would have curled into a ball on the floor, but it was sticky from spilled beverages and god knew what else.

She patted the dashboard. "This little baby takes good care of me. But damn, look at your hand. What did you do, cut it off? And why are you sitting like that? What's with you?"

I looked at the white ball of gauze making my hand three times larger than it was. "Did it cutting a bagel," I said, looking out the car window.

I hated lying to Alice.

"Jesus. You need to be more careful. I mean, you're a fucking nurse, ya know."

I shrugged. "I wonder if Rosso will give me shit about my bandage when we start orientation next week."

Alice dropped her head back and laughed, curly black hair bouncing off her glasses. "Of course Rosso will give you a hard time. That's her favorite thing about being a nurse manager. She'll find some reason to give me shit, too. I hear she does it to all new nurses. And I don't think your being the boss's daughter will save you."

She was right about that.

I peeked above the Toyota's dashboard and sank even lower.

Thank god Alice was making the new nurse journey with me. We'd met the first week of school and hit it off immediately. I'd never have made it without her. She'd studied with me, laughed and cried with me, and talked me off the ledge every time I panicked about an exam.

And, yeah, she knew about my dad. But she also knew to keep mum about it.

She even knew that my dad had pushed me into nursing school.

He'd been embarrassed of me. Plain and simple. I'd spent the better part of four years following the concert circuit, selling my handmade tie-dyed T-shirts. It wasn't a particularly well-thought-out career choice, but I loved making stuff, selling it, and especially being on the road.

It wasn't respectable, he'd said, particularly for someone from 'our world.' He and Iris liked that term, 'our world.' It was insular and exclusionary, and it reflected everything they valued.

Me, not so much.

But after they'd indulged me for as long as they could stand, they'd given me an ultimatum.

Get my ass back home and to college, or be cast out. Like they were a fucking cult.

"Are you going to tell me why you're sitting like that? You look like a paranoid nut," Alice said, her face scrunched.

I gestured with my chin toward the sidewalk. "There's the doctor who sewed up my hand. Over there"

Shit, shit, shit.

"Really? Where?" she asked, craning her neck, unbothered by discretion.

I sank lower. "Over there, crossing the parking lot now."

I peeked again, watching him make his way toward the employee parking garage, having changed from scrubs to jeans and a T-shirt.

And now that I could see him in his street clothes, my heart thumped. He'd pulled his wild hair into a sort of bun-ponytail, probably to keep it out of his face, and wore a cross-body satchel over his chest.

The way he was working that fun, hippie vibe, he could have been one of the guys on the concert circuit I'd once been part of.

Alice's eyes widened.

"Isn't he gorgeous?" I babbled.

Would she remember him from Aspen?

"He did a good job with my stitches. I didn't tell him I was a nurse, but I watched the whole procedure—"

"Oh my god," she murmured.

"I know, right, so good-looking. 'Course I lied my ass off that I wasn't related to my dad."

The car behind us beeped, signaling we'd been in the pick-up lane long enough.

Alice put the car in gear, and slowly inched out of the way. Then stopped again.

"Let's get out of here," I said.

"Oh my god," she repeated, turning to me. "You know exactly what's wrong."

I opened my eyes wide, going for an innocent look.

Not very successfully.

"We met him last year, skiing in Aspen. I know you remember," she said.

I squinted, trying to get one last look as he disappeared into the parking garage.

Alice just sat, looking at me.

I nodded.

She shook her head. "Holy shit. No freaking way."

"Yup. It's true."

4

DOCTOR BOWIE GRIER

I pulled the light blue surgical facemask I'd snatched out of the box in the doctor's on-call room over my eyes. It didn't do a great job of keeping the light out, but it was something. I could have just turned out the blinding overhead fluorescents, but it would only be a matter of time before one of my also-sleepy colleagues wandered in for a few moments of rest, flicking the lights on and banging around. It was better to fall asleep with the lights on, anyway. I wouldn't sleep as deeply, which meant it would be easier to wake up.

Five to ten minute naps were about the best an ER doc could hope for during a long shift. Although I knew

I really wasn't going to nap just then. I'd fake it, just to have a few minutes to myself, but my mind had been racing all over the damn place since my last patient.

Miss Charleigh Biddle.

Also known as Char.

Basically the woman I'd been obsessing about since our one-nighter in Aspen almost a year ago. The most mind-blowing fucking sex I'd ever had.

And to think that when I'd started stitching up her hand from a supposed 'bagel-cutting accident,' she had no freaking idea who I was.

Way to make a guy feel good.

For a moment, I thought she was pretending not to recognize me.

But then I realized she either honestly had no recollection of who I was, or she was a great actress. Given how lame her story was about how she'd put a knife through the palm of her hand, I didn't take her for a good liar. She was the type whose face was easy to read, even though she didn't want it to be read.

A year prior, I'd treated my brother and myself to a nice ski trip. After a great day of fresh powder, we'd headed to the Ajax bar, because that's what everyone did after skiing, to wind down and share stories after a day of tearing up the slopes.

It also didn't hurt that these après-ski bars were usually full of beautiful women. Beautiful, athletic women.

And just as I'd pushed my way to the bar for another locally brewed IPA, a flash of hot pink caught my attention.

It was the woman who'd ridden the chair lift in front of me on our last run of the day. She'd caught my eye in line because one, she wore a hot pink jacket that stood out in a sea of black ski clothes, and two, because her long blonde hair glinted in the afternoon sun like a blinding mirror.

Of course, all the other dudes in line were checking her out, too.

But that didn't stop me from watching where she headed when she got off the lift. I'd followed her all the way down the hill, keeping enough distance that she wouldn't think I was a stalker. She was a kick-ass skier, and in my effort to remain unseen, I lost her at a fork in the trail.

But fate intervened. There she was, standing next to me, trying desperately to get something to drink in the packed bar.

"Hey, I saw you on the lift today," I said, leaning close to be heard over the noise.

Lame opening line but what the hell.

She looked up at me with gorgeous hazel eyes. "Oh, really? Which one?"

That was how she and her friend ended up joining my brother and me. Several hours, beers, and shots of tequila later, she and I fell into bed. When she got up the next morning to pack and go home, I asked for her email on her way out.

I pinged her a couple hours later from the slopes to make sure she'd gotten to the airport okay, but her email promptly bounced back. *Invalid Address* was the message I'd gotten.

Well, shit. Guess she didn't want to keep in touch, after all.

I got it. I mean, I'd been on vacation before and done the walk of shame after spending the night out with someone I didn't want to see again. Guess I had it coming.

Someone had beaten me at my own game.

But it had eaten at me. And when I saw her in the ER, her hand swaddled in a blood-drenched towel, I couldn't believe my fucking eyes.

Char.

She'd blinked fast when I'd said her name right, something she'd told me nobody ever did. But even after that, she still had no idea who I was. At first.

What bothered me more was that her injury was most certainly *not* from cutting a bagel. I saw common household accidents all the time in the ER. They were probably fifty percent of what we treated. And a knife wound through the palm was anything but typical.

But the bottom line was that it really wasn't my business. Besides, I'd probably never see her again anyway.

"Hey. Bowie, wake up."

I pushed the facemask off my eyes. Shit. How long had I been sleeping?

Ace, my buddy from plastic surgery, sat at the end of my cot. "Dude, you put a note up on the door to wake you at noon. It's twelve-thirty."

I bolted upright and looked at my phone. "Wow. No one called me." I stumbled to the sink for mouthwash.

"Hey, did you see the new nurses touring the hospital last week? Holy fuck, are we in for some tasty delights."

Ace was a walking horndog. There was just no other way to put it.

"Buddy, if I've told you once, I've told you a hundred times, stay away from nurses. That shit leads to nothing but trouble."

He rolled his eyes. He wasn't going to listen. He never did.

Standing, he slung his backpack over his shoulder. "I'm heading out. I gotta get some sleep. Christ, I'm working around the clock. They need another plastic surgeon, but the fuckers who run this place are too goddamn cheap."

"I hear ya, bro. I'm heading out soon, too. But hey, get this. The girl I met in Aspen last year was just in here."

He raised his eyebrows. "What? That chick you

couldn't find after your one hot night of passion?" He laughed.

"Fuck off, dude. But yeah, she was in the ER. Kitchen accident. I stitched up her hand."

He nodded approvingly. "Wow. Go figure. Are you going to call her?"

I shrugged. "She had no fucking idea who I was at first, until I reminded her. Not a clue. Can you believe that?"

Ace snickered. "Guess you weren't too memorable in the sack, my friend. You'd better work on that."

He closed the on-call room's door behind him, and I heard him laughing all the way down the hall.

5

DOCTOR BOWIE GRIER

"**M**orning, Doctor," our intake clerk said when I arrived at six-thirty a.m. after a delightful weekend of rest. "Ready for a busy one?" she asked cheerfully.

How could she be cheerful about a busy ER? It usually meant people were fucked up.

Mondays in the ER were always shit. Weekend warriors of all shapes and sizes would filter in, having fallen off their roller blades, skateboards, and bikes, or who were otherwise sick and held off until Monday so they didn't mess up their weekends.

On my way to change into scrubs, one of the ER nurses grabbed me.

"Doctor Grier, we have a little kid with a pea up his nose in treatment room three."

Oh, the glamorous work of an ER doc.

"All those years of medical training for a pea," I joked. "I'll be there in five."

She laughed and hustled back to calm down what was probably a freaked-out mom and a kid just having a good time with all the attention he was getting.

Once dressed, I headed out to take care of the pea. The crowd at the nurses' station was rowdy, especially for so early in the morning. I took a slight detour toward them, in case they had cake, which they frequently did. I was hungry, even if it was only seven a.m.

But there was no early morning birthday celebration. Instead, the noise was coming from a crowd of about fifteen new nurses, who must have been the ones Ace was drooling over the day before.

I watched for a moment as the nurse in charge of orientation, Giovanna Rosso, officiously told the newbies what went on in the ER—as if they didn't already know—and that for the ones doing 'floater duty,' this was the nurses station where'd they'd check in before their shifts.

I turned on my heel as fast as I could before she dragged me into her little introduction.

But I was too late.

"Doctor Grier! Oh, Doctor Grier—"

I waved over my shoulder without turning around. "Got an emergency, Nurse Rosso. I'll catch up with you later."

I was never so grateful for a pea.

I pulled aside the curtain for treatment room three. "Mrs. Talbot, I'm Doctor Bowie Grier." I looked at her little boy, swinging his legs off the edge of the table where he sat, having a great time. "And you must be—"

"OHMYGOD, Doctor, please get this pea out of Calvin's nose before he sucks it into his sinuses or even worse, his lungs," she cried.

I didn't think she'd benefit from an anatomy lesson, so I got down to work. "Calvin, buddy. What's going on here?"

He swung his legs harder and smiled proudly. "Pea," he said simply, pointing at his nose.

"Which side, Calvin?" I asked, touching each side of his nose so he'd direct me to the right place.

He giggled and shrugged.

"Doctor, please hurry. We've been waiting so long already."

I looked at her chart. They'd arrived barely fifteen minutes ago. They were fortunate to have beaten the morning rush, which would have left them waiting hours.

But, again, I did not explain this to Mrs. Talbot.

"Okay, lie back Calvin," I said, holding his shoulders and helping him down.

But he wriggled out of my hands. "No!" he snapped.

Okay. No wonder his mother was such a wreck.

So I sat on the edge of the table, and looked at my little patient. "If you lie back like I ask, I'll get you a lollipop."

"We don't allow sweets—" his mother started to say.

But she wasn't fucking up my mojo. I cut her off. "What do you say, Calvin? Lie down for a lollipop? I'll let you pick the color."

His face brightened and he was flat on the bed before I could even finish my sentence.

Shit. I hoped we had lollipops. I wasn't actually sure we did.

I looked up Calvin's nose with a light, and unwrapped a sterile curette, a long-handled thing with a tiny scoop on the end.

"Okay, Calvin. You gonna hold still for me? For that lollipop?"

He nodded, his little face serious.

That's when I heard a chuckle. Which then turned into several chuckles.

Had his mom gone off the deep end?

I turned to look over my shoulder and saw Rosso and her group watching. I smiled and started to get back to work on Calvin when I stopped short.

What the fuck?

In the crowd of mostly female nurses, there was a familiar face. I held Calvin down with one hand and turned to get a better look.

In the back, trying unsuccessfully to hide, was a beautiful blonde wearing scrubs, her left hand bandaged up like a boxing glove.

6

CHAR

"Char?"

I ignored whoever had called my name. It was probably for some other 'Char,' anyway.

Yeah, right.

"Char?"

It was a little louder this time, accompanied by approaching steps. Alice heard them too, and I led her into the middle of our orientation group where Nurse Rosso was herding us around, in an attempt to hide.

"Char!" A hand reached through the crowd and fell on my arm.

As I turned, so did everyone else in the orientation group.

Way to make a good impression.

"Oh. Hello. I didn't see you," I lied.

Damn he was tall.

Bowie's mouth fell open slightly, like he had a hundred questions and didn't know where to start.

So I figured I'd help him out.

"Everybody, this is Dr. Grier from the ER. He stitched up my hand the other day. Dr. Grier, today is our first day at the hospital, and Nurse Rosso is giving us a tour." I gestured at the group surrounding us, in case he didn't know which one I was referring to.

About fifteen women and one guy nearly melted at his green-scrub presence. He smiled half-heartedly, and crossed his arms.

Boundaries. I liked that.

"I… just want to see how your hand was, Char."

I glanced at Rosso, who was both confused by the doctor's attention to me, and annoyed by it.

"It's okay, thank you. Just a little sore." I held it up for him to see.

He turned my bandaged hand over in his and my face grew heated from his touch. I knew I was red—in front of him and my entire orientation group, not to mention my boss.

"Why don't you come by when you're done today so I can check it?" He nodded at Rosso, turned around, and left.

Crap.

Yeah, he was more than a little surprised to find out I was a nurse in his hospital. Whoops.

We filed into the stairwell, and walked one flight down to maternity.

Alice leaned close, speaking quieter than the hushed voices surrounding us. "Guess he was gonna find out at some point. Better sooner than later, huh?" She looked at me hopefully.

She always found the silver lining in life. Hell, she *was* the silver lining in my life.

"I'm going home after work. I'm not going back to the ER. My hand is fine," I whispered. I couldn't face him. First, I'd slept with him and then, I didn't even recognize him. He probably assumed I was a big ho and did shit like that all time.

Woo-hoo! I'm on vacation! Come fuck me!

Second, I hadn't told him I was starting a job at the very hospital where he'd treated me only days before.

And to top it off, I'd lied about my dad being the head of the hospital.

Yeah, so this guy was going to think I was completely psycho. Which might not be a bad thing. At least he'd never talk to me again unless he absolutely had to.

Alice nudged me. "You can't blow him off. That would be shitty."

"Ladies, did you have a question?" Rosso asked, her lips pursed like they'd just sucked a lemon.

Everyone turned to look at us. Of course.

I shook my head, no. But Alice nodded, yes.

Oops.

"I do have a question, Nurse Rosso," she said in a serious tone, pushing her eyeglasses up on her nose. "If someone comes into the ER with an emergency delivery, are they brought up here to maternity? Or do they deliver in the ER?"

Alice tapped the side of her face with her finger, as if this were something she'd been considering for a long time.

I had to bite my tongue to keep from laughing.

And it worked. Rosso loved it.

"Wonderful question, Nurse Desjardins." She looked around at the group. "Anyone care to answer this question?"

What the hell.

I raised my hand. "I'd say they would deliver the baby in the ER since the mother's regular OB probably wouldn't have enough time to get to the hospital."

Rosso's face lit up with delight.

"Very good, Nurse Biddle. You are correct."

She clapped her hands together. "Everyone ready to see some brand-new babies now?"

My fellow nurses nodded, and the tour continued.

7

CHAR

"Char. Or should I call you *Nurse Biddle?*"

The good doctor didn't seem too happy with me. Whatever. I had no obligation to tell him anything. He could pout all he wanted

Even if I'd had great sex with him.

Really, really great sex.

I'd barely made my flight home the next morning, because I'd not gotten a wink of sleep. Alice had packed all my things, god bless her.

"You can call me either one, Doctor Grier," I said, extending my bandaged hand to him.

I caught him smirking while unwrapping the excess of bandages that made my hand so oversized.

"Call me Bowie. Any pain aside from general tenderness?" he asked, examining my sutures.

I shook my head. "Nope. Nothing an aspirin can't chase away."

And a shot of tequila. But I kept that to myself. No need to remind him of the details of that night a year ago.

When he was done wiping my palm with alcohol, he recovered the stitches, this time with a simple bandage wrapped around my hand once.

Much more manageable.

While he firmly pressed the medical tape to secure it, I tried to ward off the spreading warmth between my thighs.

I flexed my fingers. "Much better. I can fit a glove over this. Thank you."

Time to get the hell out of there. I hopped off the exam table and tossed my phone in my purse.

"Why didn't you tell me you were starting a job here?" he asked as he walked me out of the treatment room.

There it was.

People were brushing past us, crazy busy. Didn't he have better things to do than hang out with me?

I shrugged. "I was… embarrassed by my accident. I felt like a nurse should know better than to cut her hand open like I did."

His dark eyes bore into mine and he ran his fingers through his wild hair. Then, the corners of his mouth turned up like a smart-assed little smile.

Shit. I remembered that smile.

"You didn't think our paths would cross at some point?" he asked, raising his eyebrows.

I raised my hands in surrender. "Yeah. I know. It makes no sense. But I didn't know as a floater I could end up working in the ER. With you. I mean, who knew?"

Now that was about the lamest lie I'd ever told. The whole idea of being a floater nurse was to work in whatever department you were needed in, covering for nurses who were out sick or on vacation.

"Do you have any other secrets you're hiding from me?" he asked.

I giggled nervously. If he only knew.

I held my head up. "A woman is entitled to her mysteries."

He looked at me as if to say *you're full of shit*, and crossed his arms. "How'd you cut your hand again?" he demanded.

God, he was a persistent bugger.

"Bagel. I told you, I was cutting a bagel."

Shit. Why was he staring at me like that? And why did he keep asking me how I cut my hand?

"I don't know if I believe—"

I held my hand up like a *stop* sign. I'd had enough. "I'd appreciate if you'd drop it. Please," I snapped.

Surprise washed over his face. "Fine. Look, I normally wouldn't do this but here is my cell number.

Since you're going to be working here, you can let me know if you have any problems with your hand."

"Thank you."

"And if you're up for tequila shots any night, be sure to call me."

Dick.

I pulled myself together and hurried for the ER door. I was a big girl but I had to get out of there before I swooned right at his feet. Maybe I could ask Rosso to not schedule me for the ER.

I couldn't work with that man. No freaking way.

8

CHAR

"Hello," my stepmother Iris said, greeting me in the massive foyer of the massive house she and my dad lived in. "How'd you get home? I thought you were catching a ride with your dad."

Not if I could help it.

"I caught an Uber. I didn't want to wait for him. I'm exhausted." I bolted up the stairs to minimize our contact.

"Char, we have company coming over tonight," she called after me. "Can you wear that new dress I got you?"

Oh my god. How old was I, five?

I looked down over the bannister. "Iris, thanks but I'm going to bed. I can barely keep my eyes open."

Just as I spoke, the front door opened.

Dad walked in, opening his arms wide when he saw Iris. "My beautiful wife," he said, embracing her.

Perfect opportunity to sneak off to my room. But I wasn't fast enough.

"Char, get dressed. The Quinns are coming to dinner and they're bringing their son, Billy. Remember I told you about him? He's very accomplished, and he's *single*."

"He's a very nice young man, Char," Iris added.

Jesus. Were they really trying to play matchmaker? And I'd met the Quinns' son, Billy. Total. Fucking. Loser.

But I put on the dress, brushed my hair out, and swiped on some lipstick to keep the peace.

I could be a sucker that way. I wouldn't be living at their house for much longer. It was just an after-graduation way station while I got some money in the bank. I could play along for a while in exchange for free rent.

Even if I couldn't stand either one of them.

Just before our guests arrived, Dad took me aside by the arm. His hand was warm. His eyes were not.

"Now look, Char. The Quinns are very important to me. They're investing in the radiology clinic I'm developing. So please be nice."

I was sick of hearing about Dad's radiology clinic. He'd been talking about it for years, trying to do everything he could to raise the money for it. It was how he'd make his fortune he'd said over and over, as if being a hospital CEO wasn't lucrative enough.

But in reality, it *wasn't* lucrative enough—not for him and Iris. They had tastes far beyond their means. And now they were suffering for their extravagant lifestyle.

Dad was nearly broke, and he and Iris were fighting more often and more viciously. That was how I'd come to need stitches in my hand.

After an evening of too many martinis, the usual shouting match ensued. I was up in my room where I usually hid out.

When the screaming escalated, I ran downstairs to see what was happening. It turned out my father's lovely bride was chasing my dad around the kitchen, a butcher knife in her hand.

For a moment, I thought to myself, *just let her do him in.* But adrenaline got the better of me. I lunged to stop her. As she was going down, arms flailing, the blade plunged into my palm like a hot knife through butter. The room went quiet, and we watched the blood puddle on the kitchen floor. I'd done the best first aid I could, being a nurse and all, but it was clear by morning that stitches were needed.

At least I was no longer wearing the giant bandage Bowie had first wrapped me in.

I held my newly bandaged hand up to my father.

"What if they ask about this?" I asked, knowing full well it would antagonize the shit out of him.

He pressed his lips together. "You tell them what we agreed on," he hissed.

The doorbell rang and Dad released me. The Quinns breezed in with great fanfare, taking in the extravagant décor, no doubt comparing it to their own.

"Char," Mrs. Quinn purred, in a neck-and-neck race with Iris to see who had the most facial fillers.

She took my good hand and looked me up and down. "You are as beautiful as they say. You're just a vision, darling."

She spied my bandaged hand, and dropped my good one. "Goodness. What happened there?" She took a step back like I was contagious.

So I held it up to further freak her out. "Oh, it's nothing. Cut myself slicing a bagel. Hardly lost any fingers."

Needless to say, my wisecrack bombed.

After that, I said barely a word unless someone spoke to me directly, suffering through a dinner that Iris had someone come in and cook—she wasn't too talented in that area, at least not talented enough to make a good impression on the Quinns.

I was actually a pretty damn good cook, but I wasn't about to volunteer.

Their son, Billy, was seated just opposite me, no doubt planted there by both sets of parents, as if their offspring would fall in love just like they'd all become fast friends. Billy tried once or twice to engage me, but I wasn't interested in his main topic of conversation—car racing—and was so tired I was barely keeping my eyes open, anyway.

And on top of all that, I couldn't get that damn Bowie Grier out of my mind. Those crinkles around his dark eyes and his smirky grin had been spinning in my thoughts since I'd run out on him at the ER.

My hope of avoiding him at work, the more I thought about it, seemed pretty much impossible.

And I was kind of happy about that. I'd admit it.

"I'm sorry, Billy. What did you say?" I asked after I caught my father glaring at me.

Billy sighed, clearly unused to being ignored. "I said, do you want to come for a ride with me in my car?"

A ride in a car? With him?

Was he fucking kidding?

"Oh. Thanks, but I think I'll take a rain check, thank you. I started my new job today and am just pooped—"

"Oh, honey," Iris cooed, "you need a little more fun in your life. You've worked so hard on your schooling, now's the time to take a break."

She had no idea whether I'd worked hard in school. She'd never once asked about it.

Dad set down his fork and knife, always a sign he had something important to say. "Go ahead, Char. Take a little spin. Billy's got a new convertible. Put the top down and get some wind in your hair."

As if my dad's encouragement had decided everything, Billy popped to his feet and jangled the keys he'd probably been dying to pull out all night. He flashed the key fob so everyone at the table could see he had a Corvette.

Douche.

To further push me out the door, Dad got up and put his hands on the back of my chair, in a gentlemanly effort to help me out of my seat.

He never did shit like that.

"Okay, Billy," I said, defeated. "Let's go."

9

DOCTOR FLYNN MORROW

"Is that all you're having for lunch?" Bowie asked, pointing at my hard-boiled egg.

It did look a little lonely on the plate.

"Yeah. Why do you care?" I asked.

"Hey," Ace said, taking a seat at our cafeteria table, his plate loaded with possibly the biggest piece of lasagna I'd ever seen.

I pointed. "Bowie's giving me shit about my egg."

"Is that all you're eating?"

Jesus.

"I'm in training. And my mid-day meal is just this. In a few more hours, I'll eat again," I said.

Bowie picked up a fry off his own plate. "What will

you have in a couple hours? A stalk of celery? You ortho guys are always competing for something."

It was true.

I changed the subject, speaking in a lowered voice. "Don't look now but there go the new nurses," I said, glancing in the direction of the lunch line.

A gaggle of fifteen or so young women and one man had just joined the lunch line. They stood out in their clean, white sneakers, and also because they were huddled together like kittens trying to get warm.

I understood. It was intimidating as hell to start a new job, much less one in a hospital with all eyes on you.

"I'm surprised they brought in so many new ones. I thought there were budget cuts," Ace said. "There sure as hell are in plastic surgery. We're desperate for another doctor, but keep getting told no. Think of all the boob jobs we're not doing."

"Damn shame," Bowie added, craning his neck, looking.

"You see something over there you like? You're gonna end up with a crick in your neck, Bowie, staring like that," I said, finishing my egg.

"Are you gonna tell Flynn? Or should I?" Ace asked him, smirking.

He held his hand up as if to say *go ahead*.

Ace leaned closer and lowered his voice. "Remember Bowie's story about hooking up with some beautiful blonde in Aspen last year?"

Oh yeah. We'd gotten a good laugh out of that. She'd blown his ass off big time by giving him a fake email. He never should have told us because now we'd never let him live it down.

He'd acted like it was no big deal, but Ace and I could tell it bothered him. Pretty boy Bowie wasn't used to being ghosted by women.

"Sure, I remember. It's just further proof that Bowie sucks in bed," I laughed.

"Well, she's over there," Ace said, gesturing with his head.

Huh?

"What are you talking about?" I asked, watching the talkative group take up several tables in the middle of the cafeteria.

Ace drew his napkin across his mouth, his plate having been cleaned of the slab of lasagna. He ate like that all the time. Never gained an ounce. The bastard.

Bowie continued stealing glances. "You won't believe this, but she came in a couple days ago to get sutures in her hand. Had no freaking idea who I was until I reminded her. And now she fucking works here." He shook his head.

Ace stifled a laugh. "Yeah. That's the way it goes when you suck in bed."

Bowie discreetly popped Ace the middle finger.

"Seriously, Bowie. How could she just totally not recognize you?" I asked.

Sounded suspicious to me.

"Well, my hair was shorter then," he said, shrugging. "That's all I can figure."

"Okay. Say she didn't remember you. You gave her stitches. Fine. But now she works here? At Headlands Hospital? How is that even possible?"

Bowie shook his head in disbelief and lowered his voice. "I know. It's fucking crazy. I was treating a little kid who had a pea up his nose, and Giovanna Rosso comes by like a mother duck with all her new nurses in tow. They start observing me and boom, there she was, in her scrubs with her hand all bandaged up. I nearly fucking fell over."

"But did you get the pea out?" Ace asked, shaking with laughter.

Bowie rolled his eyes.

And I was speechless.

Bowie said slowly. "She's one of our new nurses. A floater. So if we're lucky, we'll all get to work with her."

Un-fucking-believable.

"Did you know she was from here, Bowie?"

He shook his head. "Nope. I knew nothing about her. Except that she was hot as shit. And could ski. And gave me a bullshit email address."

I fake-stretched over my chair back, turning in the direction of the new nurses, now getting up from their tables.

"Oh shit. Is that her? The blonde with the braid?" I asked, watching them file out of the cafeteria.

"Yup. That's her."

"I think the woman next to her with the curly hair and glasses was the friend she was with in Aspen."

No fucking way. They were *both* working at the hospital?

"That's crazy shit, man," Ace said.

I could see why Bowie was so taken with her. Not only was she stunning, but she moved with confidence, smiling and chatting with her fellow nurses.

Hell, I wouldn't mind getting to know that woman, either.

"Guys," I said. "You know my party is coming up. Maybe it's time to invite some of our new nurses."

10

DOCTOR FLYNN MORROW

I had a couple minutes to kill before a scheduled shoulder surgery, so I called my parents' house.

"Flynn? Honey?"

My mother always answered on the third ring, thinking telemarketers would have hung up by then.

"Hi, Mom."

"Your father and I were just talking about you. How's my second-favorite orthopedic surgeon?" she asked.

"Great, Mom. But I'd feel better if I were your first-favorite."

She lowered her voice to a whisper. "You know you

are my favorite, honey. I just say you're second to keep your father happy."

We all worked hard to keep my father happy. He could be a cranky old prick.

"Say, Flynn, we have a charity event coming up at the club. Why don't you join us? There are always so many nice girls there."

My mother would not rest until I had a woman in my life. She just could not comprehend why a young doctor would be single for a moment longer than he had to be.

She had no idea there was no shortage of women in my life—I just didn't share that sort of thing. I dated regularly, which Mom knew nothing about. But it was better that way, at least for the time being. She'd have me walking down the aisle with the first woman I had a second date with.

Which there probably wasn't much chance of since I had very few second dates. They just weren't my thing.

Chief among my choices were nurses. Sure, I'd been warned off dating them. It really was idiotic to go out with someone you worked with. But shit, I didn't have time to meet other women, and besides, Headlands was full of hotties. The nurses were cool about it, too, fully aware that a date did not equal a marriage proposal. Hell, they were having fun themselves, and the smart ones were in no hurry to get hitched, either.

Actually, dating nurses *had* worked out well until last year. One particular beauty from obstetrics had been unhappy when I'd not called her for a second date. She started showing up on the orthopedic floor with alarming frequency. Finally, I had to tell her to cut it out.

That didn't go over so well.

So, I was much more careful now.

"Hey, Mom, can I talk to Dad for a sec?"

"Sure, honey, but before you go, remember your brother's birthday is coming up."

My brother. Fuck me. Would I ever get to a point where those two words didn't drive a spike right into the pit of my stomach?

"Yeah. Right, mom. We'll get together and do something special to remember him."

After some muffled whispering, my father came on the line.

"Flynn?" he said, like he was addressing an audience.

Like it would be anybody else. I was their only son. Well, the only living one.

"Hi, Dad. How're you doing?"

"Fine. You?"

He was a man of few words, rarely bothered with the social expectations around small talk.

"Good, Dad, good. Hey, can I talk to you about a case?"

I pictured him sitting up in his chair, ready to dispense all sorts of wisdom.

"Of course, Flynn."

He lived for this shit now that he was retired.

"I'm looking at a case, Dad, of an eighty-eight-year-old woman needing knee surgery. She wants it, and her family wants it. The issue is, I'm concerned she might not be able to handle it."

Poor Mrs. Egan. She was cute and spunky, but terribly frail. She'd had a bad fall recently, and on top of that, had a bad heart.

My dad, before he'd retired, had been the top orthopedic surgeon in the state. So, I called on him for his insights every now and then. But his advice came not without a cost. He could be a condescending jerk.

So I braced myself.

"You know, Flynn, you shouldn't have gone into orthopedic surgery if you couldn't handle the pressure of telling patients the straight and honest truth..." he started.

Here it comes.

I'd been hoping I could get his opinion without too much of a lecture.

Today was not one of those days.

By the time he'd finished his speech, I wasn't even listening anymore, just counting the seconds before he took a breath so I could break in and say I had to go.

But nestled among his implicit and explicit insults

was a nugget of information about operating on the frail elderly.

Now I just had to find a way to tell Mrs. Egan and her family that there'd be no knee surgery.

11

DOCTOR FLYNN MORROW

I loved working on shoulders. They were the most complicated of the big joints, and while they were challenging as hell, if all went according to plan, the results were miraculous.

I had my best scrub nurse, Sunny, at my side as we worked on a college baseball player's injured shoulder.

The operating room door opened, and several people streamed in, all dressed in surgical attire.

Without looking away from my work, I leaned toward Sunny. "What's up? Visitors?" I whispered.

She glanced toward the door. "Hi, Giovanna," she called.

She leaned toward my ear. "It's Nurse Rosso with some of her newbies."

"Okay," I said.

Was Char in the group? I was too busy to look, but her pulling one over on Bowie, intentional or not, was freaking epic.

Couldn't say I blamed him for feeling stung. She was a stunner, even in her green scrubs and new white sneakers. I now knew why he was so bent over her ghosting.

"Hello, Doctor, Nurse," Rosso called across the room.

I didn't need to turn around to know she held her head up high, as if knowing Sunny and me elevated her status among her charges. She was an overbearing pain in the ass with her new nurse orientations, leading her group around like a mother hen, putting the fear of god into them for no good reason, as if they weren't already nervous enough.

"Okay, people," she said shrilly, "do not touch anything blue or green, because those items have been sterilized.

Sunny and I continued to work, while a barely perceptible hum of chatter went on behind us.

Then something metal crashed to the floor.

Goddammit.

"Nurse Biddle... Nurse Biddle, are you okay?" Rosso cried.

I glanced over my shoulder in time to see one of the

group crumple to her knees. Nurses on either side caught her arms to keep her from completely sprawling onto the floor. Her head hung slack, and a long blonde braid slipped out of her surgical cap.

Holy shit. It was Char, the very woman I'd hardly been able to take my eyes off of at lunch. The very same one who'd blown off Bowie.

"Char? Char dear, are you all right?" Rosso shrilled.

When she got no response, she barked, "Get Nurse Biddle out of here before she gets sick!"

Char was out the door in seconds, half carried, half dragged by the nurses, who still had to learn how to move patients. I had no doubt Char would have a couple nice bruises the next day.

Rosso approached the table where we were working. "My goodness. Apologies, doctor and team. We don't like to cause interruptions to your work."

"It's okay, Giovanna," Sunny said.

"Our new nurses haven't seen much surgery, obviously," she said smugly.

That was to be expected. And did she really need to have one over on brand new nurses?

Fortunately, I'd just finished the surgery. "Sunny, can you and the team clean up for me?" I asked after I'd closed up the patient's shoulder.

Taking off my gloves and mask, I ran into the hallway to see if I could find Char.

12

CHAR

"So embarrassing. In front of that cute doctor who was at lunch with Bowie, not to mention Rosso and the whole orientation group."

I hung my head in my hands.

Alice rolled her eyes. "Oh, relax. Get over yourself. In a few days, nobody will remember you passed out watching a surgery."

She was trying not to laugh. And I was trying not to kill her.

"Besides, we were covered in surgical attire. We're basically unrecognizable." She poured me more tea, which I brought to my face to inhale the steam.

I hadn't been wild about the idea of going to a

coffee shop so close to the hospital—the place could be crawling with staff from Headlands—but it was quick and easy, and I needed to calm my nerves before I went home to the shitshow that was my stepmom and dad, and listened to them rave about Billy.

"No one might have recognized me, but when the lovely Nurse Rosso called out my name, that sure as hell cleared up any uncertainty. I just don't know what happened. I've never fainted. But when I saw him start manhandling that shoulder joint like he was trying to stuff a too-big suitcase in an overhead bin, I felt myself going down."

This was not a good sign. Nurses can't freaking faint. And that ortho surgeon—what if I had to work with him?

Scratch that *if*. Of course I'd have to work with him.

Brand new on the job and already humiliated myself.

I ran my fingers over the bandage on my hand. The stitches would come out in another week. Which meant I'd get to see Bowie, if I didn't before then.

Wait a minute. I was supposed to be avoiding him.

"Does anyone know who your dad is yet?" Alice asked in a quiet voice.

Another thing weighing on my mind.

I looked around for eavesdroppers. Yeah, I was paranoid.

"Rosso knows. She made a comment the other day, insinuating that's how I got my job."

Alice rolled her eyes. "Such a witch."

Rosso had been flat-out wrong, and I'd tried to convince her I'd been hired via a competitive selection process. But what was particularly distressing was how she didn't hesitate to voice her assumption directly to me.

Who does that?

Most of the graduates of my nursing program ended up at Headlands because it was so big and they always needed nurses. But the truth was, I hadn't even wanted to work there, in part because my dad ran the place, and also because I preferred working with an under-resourced population, like the patients they got at County Hospital. When I expressed interest in going elsewhere, my father smacked that thought down before I'd even finished my sentence.

And I knew why. He wanted to keep an eye on me, plain and simple. I didn't know *why* then, but I did now.

Dad and Iris had been running out of money for some time. Sure, hospital CEOs made bank—certainly more than I'd ever make in my lifetime as a nurse.

But a couple semesters before graduation, the tuition check my dad had written to the university bounced. The school sent a letter to me since I was the student, and told me that if my account wasn't paid in full in ten days, I was to leave. As in, get the hell out. I freaked, not because I couldn't pay it myself—I had just enough savings in my account from my part-time job on campus—but because it provided some visibility into my dad's world that I hadn't had before.

I'd decided to run home for a chat with my dad in person, driving my then-running Prius. But when I arrived, Dad and Iris were going at it in one of their infamous shouting matches. It was clear to me—and to most everyone except my dad—that she'd married him for his money, and was now going through every bit she could get her hands on. Further running down their resources, they spent a lot of time, probably too much, hanging out with the hospital's board of directors, a bunch of rich philanthropists if ever there was one.

I mean, there was rich and then there was mega-rich. As much as my dad and Iris tried to fool themselves, they were *not* mega-rich. The private jets they hired and castles they rented in European countries to impress their highbrow friends had sucked up all their credit.

Out of necessity, they'd finally gradually tightened their belts. They dropped their country club membership, which they never used anyway, and let the household staff go, one by one.

At first, I thought they'd spent themselves into oblivion out of vanity. A need to belong to a group they weren't members of, the same way they'd joined a country club that they never used. But in between their screaming matches, I found the real reason they were trying to impress the uber-high rollers.

Dad was trying to raise money for that damn radiology clinic. They were supposedly very profitable, and there was nothing like it in our area.

So, he'd made a calculated risk by investing in friendships with the richest people he could find, in the hopes that it would pay off in spades.

Yeah, good luck with that.

Enter the Quinns.

I was guessing they were his last hope. If he could help their pathetic son Billy find a decent woman, so much the better. So yeah, in my dad's eyes, I was currency. Very valuable currency.

And that's why he needed to keep a close eye on me.

I'd known for a long time, really since my mom had split, not to expect much from my dad, but this latest bullshit of pushing Billy on me was beyond the pale. I was really dying to share the drama with Alice, but pride was holding me back. She already knew I was a fuck-up late bloomer who'd rather be selling crap outside concert venues.

But that was my past and I needed to forget about it. I was *responsible* now.

Right.

13

CHAR

"How's orientation going?" Dad asked off-handedly while he steered his big-ass Mercedes onto the freeway.

Was the car just another thing he could ill afford?

"Good. We toured surgery today, and I got to see part of a shoulder repair."

I left out the part about my fainting.

"But you know, Dad, I was thinking again that I might like to apply for a job at County. I really like the idea of working with the underprivileged."

Plus, I could get away from my humiliating past with Bowie Grier.

Without missing a beat, he shot me down like he

always did. "Absolutely not. Hospitals like that are filthy. You'll catch things you've never even heard of from the patients there."

How did someone like him end up in the healthcare business? His heart was as cold and black as they came.

He had no compassion for patients and no respect for the hospital employees. And when I wondered how he'd managed to keep his job there for so many years, I recalled how he'd snowed the board of directors.

Were they that stupid?

"Billy's coming over tonight to see you," Dad said in a tone indicating it was a 'done deal.' No sense in arguing. Next subject.

But no one had ever accused me of being particularly sensible.

"Dad, I am so tired I want to cry. I'm going right to bed after I have a snack—"

"Like hell you will. I need you to charm Billy, Char. Our future depends on the Quinn family."

Our future?

"I really can't, Dad, I'm sorry. I'm so tired."

He smiled smugly, reminding me of Nurse Rosso's self-important proclamations. "You have to learn to get by with little sleep. You're a medical professional now."

He might run a hospital, but he had no idea what it was like to be sleep-deprived.

"I'm sorry. I can't."

He pulled off the freeway and came to a screeching halt on an off-ramp.

"Dad, is this a safe place to be stopped?" I asked, looking behind us to see what speeding car was going to be the cause of our death.

He shook a finger in my face.

Really?

"The Quinns are investing in my radiology business. They've verbally committed to it. But I won't relax until I see some money from them. A lot of money. So if their son Billy likes you, you better damn well like him back."

What fucking century was he living in? Did people still marry to please parents and bind alliances?

"I'm sorry, Dad, but that guy is a loser."

His face turned ugly and red. "You think you're so special?" he bellowed in my face.

And there it was. I was expendable. Just another asset.

I had to get the fuck away from him and Iris. My plan to camp out and live rent free for a month had just proven unworkable.

Dad hadn't always been a selfish prick. But when my mother left us years earlier, the man I'd always adored left, too.

He took a deep breath. "Char," he started to say, this time in a calmer tone, "I didn't mean that. I'm sorry. But do you want to be responsible for Iris's and my misery? We have an incredible business opportunity in front of us. It's going to be hugely profitable in no time. We need this."

I said nothing. Just stared straight ahead.

"Hey, Billy," I said, completely without enthusiasm.

"Char, you look great," he said, looking me up and down without an ounce of discretion.

There was nothing sadder than a guy who thought he was *all that*, and just wasn't. And he was full of shit, besides. I was wearing a cheap T-shirt dress from Old Navy and my Converse chucks. It was the same outfit I might wear to take out the trash.

"Darling," Iris clucked, kissing Billy on both cheeks like she'd just arrived off a flight from France.

She loved to put on a show.

She waved with her fingertips. "We're on our way out. You kids have the place to yourself. Have fun," she said with a little giggle.

Gross.

Would it be weird to beg them not to go?

Iris took Dad's arm, and they headed out the door. Dad waved over his shoulder and they were gone.

I just wanted to cry.

But Billy looked thrilled, surely thinking he was going to get some.

"Do you have anything to drink?" he asked like an underage kid who had to sneak booze.

"Yeah. Follow me."

I led him to the library, which had a full bar. I

gestured and told him to help himself while I poured myself a small glass of wine.

I needed to keep my wits about me.

He helped himself to Dad's expensive scotch.

"You know, you don't look anything like your mother."

"Iris is not my mother—"

But he interrupted. "You can usually get an idea of what a girl's going to look like when she gets older by looking at her mother. Yours doesn't look so great, which is really surprising because you're pretty hot."

He did *not* just say that.

"First, Billy, Iris is not my mother. My mother split when I was little."

"Ooooh, that's right," he said, realization washing over his blank face.

"And second, that's a shitty way to talk about women."

He looked confused. "I was just trying to pay you a compliment."

That's true. That *was* all he was doing. And he'd never understand that in doing so, he was seven levels of wrong.

Untrainable was what he was.

So I faked a sneeze. A big one. I may have even sprayed a little.

I pretended to wipe my nose with my sleeve. "Oh damn. I hope I'm not coming down with anything. I was in pediatrics today, and those poor little kids are so sick…" I lied.

Billy looked horrified and inched away. "Um. Are you serious? That's disgusting."

He set his drink down and stood. "I gotta hit the road. I forgot I have an errand to run."

And he was gone.

I breathed a deep sigh of relief, impressed with myself and grateful for my little victory. I drank the last of my wine, and headed upstairs to bed.

I was setting the alarm on my phone after I'd gotten under my covers when a text came through.

doctor grier here

Oh. Shit. What did he want? I debated not answering. I could pretend I was already asleep. But it was only nine p.m., and he'd know I was bullshitting him. Again.

hi doctor grier, I texted.

actually, call me bowie

ok bowie

how's the hand? he asked.

kind of sore

want me to take a look at it?

do you offer this kind of service to all your patients? I asked.

smart ass. offer rescinded

fine. didn't mean to hurt your feelings.

This was kind of fun. Conversing with someone who had a brain. That's how low Billy had set the bar.

MIKA LANE

i have a party this weekend. want to come? he asked.

Oh god no. Spending time with this man would lead to nothing but trouble.

Sure. okay, I replied.

Oh my god. Were my fingers possessed? Didn't I already have enough problems? And what party? I needed details.

But I didn't ask for them. I just said good night.

I should have been thinking of a reason to back out of Bowie's party. Instead, I fell asleep with a smile on my face.

First time in a long time.

14

DOCTOR ACE HARDIN

"**I** got out of the Army to *get away* from arrogant assholes like Cole."

I helped myself to the seat opposite Bowie's desk.

He looked up from the patient notes he was working on. "Ace, if you wanted to get away from arrogant people, you chose the wrong speciality, my friend."

Plastic surgeons were famous for being dicks, Bowie was right. When I accepted my position at Headlands, I knew what I was walking into. What I didn't expect was a bureaucracy that protected doctors who were past their prime, and whose skills were slipping.

Like the venerable Doctor Cole, the senior surgeon in my department.

I had the US Army to thank for my excellent training. But when my days in the field turned into nothing more than the soul-killing patching up of broken kids who'd been sent to war by old men, things started to go sour.

I repaid my debt to the government for financing my education and got out first chance I got.

Every job has its share of problems, and my position at Headlands was no different—except now I wasn't dealing with injured and dying young men.

Without the trauma work of the military, my life now had a more predictable rhythm. By all accounts, it was a step in the right direction. No more waking up in the middle of the night seven days a week to put together some young kid who'd been blown to bits.

But in some ways working with someone like Cole was even worse. "Bowie, I pointed out to him during a procedure that we might try a different approach, and he exploded. He took my suggestion, but still dressed me down in front of the entire surgery team. What a hypocrite."

Bowie's eyes widened, and he sat back, arms crossed. "No way. What a prick. He realized you were right and ripped you a new asshole anyway?"

"Yeah. It was all for show. To prove to everyone in the room that he was top dog."

I shuddered to think what the outcome might have

been, had I kept my mouth shut. But it certainly wouldn't have been good for the patient. And if it wasn't good for the patient, it wasn't good for anyone.

"You have to report him to the Chief Physician, Ace," he said.

I nodded. Bowie had been at Headlands longer than I had and knew what he was talking about.

"I hate this shit," I said.

"I know. We all do. But it's part of the job, man."

I put my head in my hands.

"Hey, how's your brother?" Bowie asked.

I looked up. That was a good question.

"I gotta call him later today. But I think he's getting out in the next year. Hope so."

"Oh man. That would be great. I've never met him," Bowie said.

Jesus. He was right. Bowie and I had been in medical school and trained together, but my brother hadn't been around for any of it.

He sat back in his chair, a shit-eating grin across his face. "I got some news."

Must be good.

"I invited someone to Flynn's party."

Well, I'll be damned. And I'd bet one hundred dollars I knew just who he'd invited.

"Your friend from Aspen? The one who fainted in Flynn's surgery yesterday?"

He burst out laughing. "No way. She fainted? Poor thing." Bowie shook his head.

Fainting happened in the medical profession from time to time, so we could empathize. But that didn't mean she wouldn't get major ribbing over it for a long time to come.

"Apparently Flynn had a shoulder surgery underway and Rosso had some of her group observing. He heard someone go down, and who was it but the pretty blonde."

"Ugh. That must have sucked," Bowie groaned.

"I'm sure Rosso made it more miserable than it had to be," I added. "Anyway, glad you invited her. I'd like to get to know her better, myself."

With a single nod, he confirmed he knew just what I was thinking.

I was hoping he'd make a move on the beautiful new nurse.

We all did.

15

DOCTOR ACE HARDIN

"Ace. Hey, little bro. What's up?" my brother Dillon asked.

I could hardly hear him with all the racket in the background. Prisons were noisy places. But I knew that well. My brother had been in prison so long I barely remembered him on the outside.

"How are ya?" I asked, steering into traffic on my way to play ball with the guys and some of the new medical residents.

He sighed. "I'm hanging in. Only another year or so, if the parole board sees through to releasing me."

My heart thumped. Dillon wanted out, and I wanted him out. He was going to start over, and I was going to help him. His life had been one raw deal after another, and all I wanted was to see him get a break or two.

"Dil, stay on the straight and narrow man, and it will happen. Your room in my place is ready to move into. All we have to do is get your ass there."

He started to say something, but his voice broke.

I got it.

After a moment, he cleared his throat that way guys do when they're trying to play it cool. "Thanks, Ace. I don't know what I'd do without you."

My throat caught, too. "You won't be saying that when you're out. I'm still a slob. And I snore loud enough to shake the house."

"All right, little bro. You convinced me. I'll stay in the slammer because it's so clean and quiet here."

He laughed, a sound I hadn't heard from him in a long time. When he got out, I planned for a lot more of that.

Dillon and I, we'd grown up on the wrong side of opportunity. But that in itself wasn't a death sentence, absolutely not. I had a teacher who believed in me, and got me to study, much like Bowie had. In fact, our lives had been so similar we'd bonded as soon as we'd met in med school. But my brother Dillon was a different story. Even though he was actually the smart one, he'd made the mistake of falling in with the wrong crowd. One night, outside a bar, he got into a fight. He hit his opponent just so, and the guy fell, hitting his head on a concrete step. He died, and Dillon went to prison.

I continued with college.

Dillon had potential. It was just that no one ever took the time to tell him, like they had me. When he got out, I was going to be the advocate he'd never had.

"Hey, how many people at the hospital where you work know you have an incarcerated brother?"

I hesitated. But I knew he'd understand. "Just my closest buddies, Bowie and Flynn. It's nobody else's business."

He chuckled. "I'd handle it the same way, little bro. I don't blame you."

But for the grace of god…

Next day during my rounds, who did I find but Char administering to one of my elderly patients. Perfect timing. Bowie had encouraged me to talk to her, and I'd been waiting for the opportunity.

"Well, well. It looks like we got a party going on here," I said, walking over to my patient and gently squeezing her arm.

Char looked up, surprised. "Oh. Sorry, Doctor. Let me finish up here so you can chat with Mrs. Herron."

I watched her help the woman get more comfortable by adjusting the bed, adding and subtracting pillows, and providing an extra blanket to ward off a chill. She was patient, confident, and moved slowly, stopping to make sure and smile at the patient.

I loved that.

"Take your time, please," I insisted.

I did want her to take her time. I was enjoying the hell out of watching her. She was more stunning than ever as she carried out her work. Her glossy hair was twisted into a neat confection at the nape of her neck, and her curves—not easy to see under shapeless scrubs —were the stuff men dream about.

Shit, I could have watched her all day.

"There we go, Mrs. Herron," she said, bending to touch the patient's arm again. "It's Doctor Hardin's turn to visit with you now."

The patient, while a bit on the woozy side, smiled up at Char like she was a freaking angel.

Didn't blame her.

I got to work asking Mrs. Herron how she was getting on when a rustling behind me caught my attention. I turned and found Char watching from the doorway. When she realized she'd been caught, she gave me the sexiest crooked smile and took off.

I patted Mrs. Herron's arm. "You are doing amazingly well. Keep up the good work." I quickly excused myself.

With a bit of jogging, I caught up to Char. "Thanks for your work back there. You did a great job."

Her eyes brightened. "Really? Thanks."

"By the way, I'm Ace Hardin. Bowie told me you're

coming to Flynn's party this weekend. We'll all go together, okay?"

Surprise washed over her face. "Oh. Sure. That would be great. You know Bowie?"

Fuck, she was beautiful.

"Yeah, we're friends. He pointed you out in the cafeteria the other day. Said you're dangerous with knives and bagels."

She gave me another of those crooked smiles. "He's right. I am."

The more I thought about it, the more I thought County Hospital, with its underserved population, would be a better fit for me. I could stand only so many breast enhancements, nose jobs, and tummy tucks. I wanted to impact the lives of those needing cleft palate surgery, burn scar repair, and trauma reconstruction.

I reached out to one of my medical school professors, whom I'd become friends with over the years, for his opinion.

"What do you think I should do?" I asked.

He took a long inhale. "The position you have right now is very prestigious."

It very well may have been, but prestige was not something I was after.

He knew me well enough to know my priorities. "But you have to go where you feel you can make the biggest difference. That's what makes you happy, Ace. Not money or status."

I didn't come from money, so I didn't really care how much of it came my way or not. That wasn't what got me up in the morning. Not that I wanted to be as poor as Dillon and I had been growing up. But my needs were simple. My wants were minimal.

"Ride it out for a while. Don't make any hasty decisions. When is your contract there up?" Charles asked.

"Less than a year."

"Well, there's your answer. You can't do anything for a while, anyway. That'll give you time to assess whether or not Headlands is the right place for you."

"Thanks, Charles."

I might have been unsure about Headlands, but if I had to spend another year there, at least it would be in the company of friends… and the lovely Char.

16

CHAR

It was like I was in fucking middle school again. I actually had to sneak out of the house while Dad and Iris were having drinks in the library and grab an Uber since my car still was not 'repaired.'

Alice said I needed to move the hell out of Dad and Iris's house. She was right. As soon as I had first month's rent and my deposit saved up, I would. I'd managed to graduate without a penny to my name, having spent my savings on tuition because dad had run out of money. But I'd be in the black soon.

When I did hit the road on Dad and Iris, I foresaw a blow up of epic proportion. I could see it now. Dad would threaten to cut me out of the will like he always did. Tell me I'd be responsible for his downfall, and cause my stepmother and him a lifetime of wretchedness.

And, he'd *cut me out of the will*. What a joke. He didn't have a penny to his name. Or so he claimed.

His guilt trips had worked wonders on me for years. I fell for every single one. But those ties and obligations were coming to a quick end.

Just another month. Maybe a little more. That would be it. I'd be out of their tacky-ass mansion.

And with that departure would be the end of tolerating Billy. Once I was gone, they could all fuck off.

The day couldn't come soon enough.

My dad had manipulated my long-suffering sister Franny, just like he had me, who'd bowed to his every demand. She'd ended up marrying the guy Dad had pressured her to, and now lived out in the burbs with a baby.

Her life wasn't horrible by any means. But she'd given up her dream of singing even though she'd attended a top music school.

For the longest time, we thought he was pushing us because he had our best interests at heart.

But when I started to see how he and Iris pretended to be something they were not, I began to watch them more closely.

My Uber dropped me at a cool old building that had not long ago been turned into loft style condos.

Damn. Flynn was doing well for himself.

And I was about to make an entrance at his party. Ace and Bowie had wanted to pick me up, but of course I made an excuse. Another lie. But I couldn't have them come to my dad's house.

Cripes. What was I getting myself into, attending a party with my one-night stand from a ski vacation? Did he invite me because he thought he might get some? That I'd rip my panties off the moment he asked?

It was probably what he was accustomed to. But he'd quickly learn that what we'd done is Aspen was a fluke. Just because I'd fucked him once, didn't mean it was going to happen again.

No matter how gorgeous he was.

I took a deep breath and headed up the crunchy gravel path to the speakerphone outside Flynn's building. After I identified myself, I was buzzed into a lobby of glass, concrete, and orchids. I pressed the elevator button for the third floor.

To my surprise, it opened right into a gigantic apartment full of people who were drinking, eating, and smiling.

An elevator direct to his apartment. That was some serious swank.

Bowie saw me before I saw him and headed my way with a broad smile, adorable with his unruly curls pulled back into a ponytail. "I would have picked you up," he said, grinning. "How's the hand?"

He picked it up and turned it over.

"Aren't you off-duty, Doctor Grier?" I teased.

Or was I flirting?

Shit. I figured since I'd gone through the trouble of sneaking out of Dad's house, I might as well make the most of it.

And as if he could read my mind, Bowie held on to my hand. I smelled danger, and I'd willingly walked right into it.

The *good* kind of danger

"I'm off duty for patients. But you aren't a patient."

Why? Because we'd been naked together?

He was flirting with me just like he had in Aspen. How had I not immediately recognized this gorgeous man when he'd stitched up my hand that day in the ER? Those same smiling eyes that had charmed me before were working their magic on me again.

Only this time, things were even more intense. I'd seen the man in his element. I'd seen how kind he was with his patients. I'd seen him dead tired but still willing to smile at someone who was sick and afraid.

He was more appealing now by a factor of ten. Which scared the crap out of me.

And the way he was holding my hand on the pretense of examining it was making my heart pound.

"Ah, here she is," a sexy voice crooned.

I turned to see Ace extending me a glass of champagne.

Wow. How did he know?

"Thank you, Doctor Hardin," I said, our fingers brushing each other's as he handed me my glass.

He was every bit as handsome as Bowie, but more in a Prince Harry sort of way with spiky red hair and light facial scruff. He was nearly as tall as Bowie, his pecs stretching the limits of the blue button-down he wore, which was cuffed up to just below his elbows, revealing some badass looking tattoos.

To hide my nerves, I took a long draw from my flute. Holy cow. Flynn was serving the good stuff. There were some valuable things I'd learned from my father's years of extravagance. Fortunately for me, that included appreciating good food and wine.

Seemed like Flynn subscribed to that same school of enjoying life's finer things.

"Char, you can call me Ace. Please. I enjoyed seeing you work with that patient the other day."

"Thank you. She was sweet. I hope she makes out okay." I'd been enjoying watching him work, too, until he'd caught me staring.

The heat running through my veins at that moment was enough to make me want to tear my clothes off. I was confronted with two of the most beautiful men I'd ever seen.

I finished my champagne. Not a good move. I needed to keep my wits about me.

"Are you checking out my scar?" Ace asked, pointing to a faded line above his lip.

That wasn't all I was looking at. I glanced at Bowie, who seemed amused by my state of agitation.

"Sorry. I was staring."

He and Bowie looked at each other and laughed.

"Is that from a bike wreck when you were a kid?" I asked.

He nodded. "Sure is. The telltale bike wreck scar."

What a contrast these guys were to Billy, who had himself all bulked up due to his short man's syndrome, and who shaved his head to hide the fact that he was balding.

I spotted Flynn across the room and waved. He made his way over, making hellos and patting people on the back as he moved through the crowd with the fluidity of a big cat in the wild, outrageously elegant with his prematurely silver hair and clean-shaven face.

He looked at his buddies, then me, his piercing blue eyes holding my attention hostage. Holy shit. How did the universe make three such flawless men, put them all in one room together, and gather them around *me*?

"Glad you could make it, Char. Welcome. Looks like you're ready for a refill." Even his chin dimple was perfection.

I was tongue-tied. I wanted to thank him for inviting me. Tell him his place was amazing. Show him I wasn't a total dolt who went around passing out at work.

"Hey, I hope you're feeling better than the other day," he said, genuine concern crossing his face.

He was concerned about *me*? Some piss-ant nurse who nearly barfed as he worked miracles on a college athlete's shoulder?

"Oh my god, so embarrassing," I said, looking at them all. Their eyes were so kind and friendly, such a contrast to the way Billy looked at me, that my confidence came seeping back.

So I resorted to a little humor.

I moved closer to the guys, like I was sharing a secret. They followed my lead, gathering closer.

"My plan is to faint in each department to really piss off Nurse Rosso."

"Cheers to that," Flynn said, and we all clinked glasses. He spotted some new guests arriving via his personal elevator. "I'm off to circulate, but please make yourself at home, Char."

"What about us, man?" Ace asked, looking fake hurt.

"Dude, you're lucky you were even invited," Flynn laughed.

He wandered off, adoring female gazes following him and his athletic ass.

Including mine.

"How are you enjoying Headlands?" Ace asked, his green eyes giving me heart palpitations.

"Well…"

I considered how to answer that without the question of whether I was the CEO's daughter coming up. By now he knew my last name was Biddle, and he was probably just being polite in not coming right out and asking. Sure, he and the rest of them would eventually find out, but hopefully not until after I'd proved myself.

"It's great," I said simply. "How do you like it?"

Bowie and Ace looked at each other.

"It's working for me," Bowie said.

I turned to Ace. "Time will tell. I'm not sure whether it's the place for me in the long run."

He stepped closer, his lips near my ear.

God, did he smell good.

"But let's keep that between us for now," he said. "I don't need my boss to know I may not be there for the duration."

"My lips are sealed."

God knew I was dragging around a shit ton of secrets.

"Hi, guys," the nurse from Flynn's surgery said, sticking her chest out and ignoring me.

Really? Is that how she wanted to be?

"Hey, Sunny," Bowie said, ignoring her tit-thrust.

I looked directly at her. "I'm gonna take a lap. Looks like there's some good sushi over there." I gestured toward a table stacked high with food.

I popped a couple California rolls in my mouth, and as I suspected, they were heavenly. Flynn didn't buy cheap grocery store shit. I passed on the sashimi, though. I didn't need to spend the night with fish breath.

And now that I'd taken a breather from the distraction of the guys, I was able to appreciate Flynn's insanely modern loft apartment. It was such a far cry from the traditional décor at my dad's house, where every nook and cranny was crammed with some sort of item in another shade of brick red.

Flynn's place was all soaring ceilings hanging with giant industrial lights straight out of an old school factory. Not surprisingly, the kitchen was full of sleek stainless steel, giving it a kind of spaceship high tech look. The living room, with lots of open space and fluffy rugs scattered over a polished concrete surface, was dotted with low-to-the-floor sofas and chairs. Everything was black, white, and gray with the exception of a couple fur throw pillows in bright orange.

I'd never seen anything like it. Personally, I preferred warmer interiors, but I could admire Flynn's place for what it was—expensively and beautifully decorated.

Given that it was a loft, of course there was a wide-open staircase leading someplace my nosy ass was dying to see. I looked around, and with Bowie and his friends occupied with other guests, figured I'd give myself a tour.

I was halfway up the stairs when I stopped.

"—how did she get invited?" Someone clucked her tongue.

"Yeah, how does a brand-new nurse, who doesn't know anyone or anything, get invited to a party like this? What's her name? Cher? Like the singer?"

She was close with my name. That never happened.

"Something like that. Probably just another gold-digger. Got into nursing to meet a rich doc. Wait till she finds out what assholes most of them are…"

They erupted into giggles.

Guess I wouldn't be seeing the upstairs. I turned to head back down.

Wait.

Fuck those bitches. They weren't going to chase me off. I'd been invited just like they had.

I fluffed my hair and stretched to full height, stomping up the wooden steps right towards them.

When they saw me, the smug slipped right off their faces.

But I smiled bravely. "Just so you know, ladies, for when we work together—and I know we will soon—my name is pronounced *Char*."

I smiled and met the gaze of each, including the creep who'd ignored me downstairs.

She looked at me with wide eyes. "Oh, um, we weren't talking about you—" she started to say.

But I stepped through the middle of their group, forcing each one to take a step back to make way. "I'll just continue my tour. Isn't this place awesome? I've never seen anything like it."

Adrenaline surging, I took in the room, along with some deep breaths. Those sad, gossipy women weren't going to ruin my evening.

Wait until they found out I was the CEO's daughter. Then they'd really hate me.

My heart still pounding, I wandered through an office of some sort and down a small hallway where I found Flynn's bedroom. Like a typical guy room, and the rest of the house, really, it was decorated in grays, with a huge black and white painting over the bed. In the far corner was an en suite bathroom I was dying to check out. But I didn't want to barge into his bedroom. At least not without being invited first.

I went back downstairs where I noticed an open door off the kitchen. I wove through the smartly dressed crowd, happy to find the gossipy nurses were nowhere in sight.

Through the kitchen door was another staircase, this one leading to a rooftop deck.

What a place.

As I climbed the stairs, hoping I wouldn't overhear another group of people talking about me, I spotted Bowie on the far side of the deck. He was talking to some woman. Very closely.

Maybe I should have just stayed at home.

17

CHAR

I quietly headed back to the kitchen, when I ran smack into Ace.

His eyes brightened when he saw me. I instantly felt better. "Char! Did you check out the view from the roof? Is this place fucking awesome, or what?"

What the hell. Why should I run away from Bowie cozying up to some woman? Yeah, he was hot, and I was pretty sure he'd flirted with me, but it wasn't like we had anything going on.

Well, I'd slept with him too.

"Let's go."

Just as we reached the top, the woman Bowie had been talking to rocketed down the stairs past us, forcing us to jump aside to avoid being trampled.

Guess their talk hadn't gone well.

"Hey, brother," Ace called out to Bowie, now standing alone, gazing into the distance.

"Here she is," Bowie said, smiling at me. Even in the dark I could see the sexiness in his eyes. "Flynn's place is so big I figured you'd gotten lost. Or made some new friends."

Not exactly…

Ace clapped Bowie on the shoulder. "Dude, was that woman who just bolted out of here Sandi? The one who's been bugging you?"

Bowie shifted uncomfortably. "Yeah. I had to be firm this time and tell her we were a no-go."

Interesting. Was he saying that just for my sake? I didn't mean to flatter myself, but hell, he'd invited me to the party.

"Hadn't you already had that conversation with her?" Ace asked.

Bowie glanced at me, embarrassed. Guess Ace was not as diplomatic as he might be.

"Several times. I think I got the message across this time, though."

"Is that an old girlfriend?" I asked. I was curious. And nosy.

"Oh no," he said, shaking his head. "She… has been quite persistent. But it's not gonna happen. She's not my type."

Oh.

"But," he said slowly, his gaze drilling into mine, "*you* are."

Me?

I was his type? The man didn't beat around the bush. And right in front of Ace, no less.

I shifted in my boots, a sound coming out of my throat that was supposed to sound like a casual laugh. But it came out as more of a strangled cough.

Bowie looked at his friend. "Ace is interested in you, too, Char."

Um, what?

The corner of Ace's mouth turned up in a heated stare, and he rubbed at the scruff on his chin, drawing attention to that damn dimple.

So freaking cute.

But Bowie's comments were well beyond flirting. Were these guys propositioning me? Were they kinky *ménage à trois* dudes?

I'd had a threesome in college, and it had been pretty fucking hot. I might be open to another...

A little voice was singing *but you work with these guys.*

I muzzled it pretty quickly.

Ace took one of my hands, and Bowie gently took the one that was bandaged.

Hot threesome, here I come.

"You know how beautiful you are, darlin'?" Ace asked, kissing my hand.

Wow, Doctor Hardin, gorgeous Headlands Hospital plastic surgeon, making the moves on me.

Surprised? Yes. Complaining? Hell no.

Bowie took a step closer, his foot touching mine as if to throw me off balance, and brought a hank of my hair to his face. "Goddamn. Smells so good."

I wanted to play it cool, but my gaze whipsawed from one guy to the other. I couldn't decide who I should be looking at. I couldn't decide who I *wanted* to be looking at.

Kid in a candy store never rang truer...

While my gaze whipsawed, so did my equilibrium. Or lack of it.

I had so many questions.

Had they planned this?

Was I just their target?

Or were they really interested in me?

And were they aware that so much of what they knew about me was based on lies?

Bowie leaned closer, as I'd hoped he would, until I could feel his breath, scented by mint and expensive scotch. Up close, his flawless skin was speckled by a beard shaved several hours earlier, returning to make its evening appearance.

Unable to tolerate his tease any longer, I pressed my mouth to his. He responded in kind, parting his lips just enough to flick me with his tongue.

Watching, Ace groaned quietly.

I was kissing Bowie just like I had back in Aspen.

When we'd been there, I'd felt free to do whatever the hell I wanted in the knowledge that I was on vacation and would never see him again.

Or so I'd thought.

My current situation, while just as charged with need, was so much more complicated. *Only an idiot gets involved with people at work*, kept flashing through my mind, like a banner being pulled behind a slow-moving airplane over a sports stadium. But on the other hand, the attraction buzzing around the three of us was not just some horny, hormonal impulse.

I placed one hand on the side of Bowie's face, and the other on Ace's, turning to him, the handsome redhead I'd watched from a distance all week.

Ace didn't wait for me to kiss him first. Instead, his lips crashed into mine, soft for a moment, then aggressive. They revealed a breathtaking hunger, the kind every woman hopes for in a man.

It made me feel beautiful. Wanted. Powerful.

And it helped me forget the crazy darkness that had been infringing on the new, post-college life I was trying to build.

These guys were fucking hot. I was not turning them away.

With one hand still on Bowie, I reached an arm around Ace's neck, falling into his kiss—

"Well. What have we here?"

I screeched.

Footsteps approached and my adrenaline exploded, urging me to flee some sort of danger.

Could I hide? Maybe jump off the roof?

Instead, I turned to see who it was.

There stood Flynn, stopped in his tracks, holding his hands up. "Whoa, whoa, Char. Didn't mean to startle you."

Oh my god. We were busted.

I probably needed to get home, anyway.

"Flynn," I croaked, releasing the guys and taking a step back from them.

Nothing to see here, folks...

Oh god, oh god, oh god.

"Hey... Flynn. I was just... um... talking with the guys," I said, pointing at Bowie and Ace as if there were someone else around.

Flynn stuffed his hands in his pockets and nodded slowly, his ice blue eyes tormenting me. "Char, honey, I'm not sure I believe you. In fact, I think you might be telling me a little lie right now."

Fuck. He'd seen everything. Was I going to get in trouble? What if he told Rosso?

Maybe I could talk him into being cool.

With pleading eyes, I looked to Bowie and Ace for help. But they just stared back with the slightest smiles on their faces.

Fuckers. They'd set me up. I knew it.

God I was stupid.

Maybe I could convince Flynn he'd seen nothing. I could lie. I was good at that.

"Flynn, seriously, we were just hanging out, nothing more than that—"

But before I could finish, his mouth closed on mine. His hands took my face to pull me closer, and he kissed me with a fury that left me shaking more than I already was.

"Oh," I murmured, touching my lips when he'd let me go.

"Oh, we forgot to tell you one thing," Bowie said. "Flynn likes you, too."

18

CHAR

I grabbed a banana before I went to wait out in front of the house for Alice to pick me up.

Before I escaped the kitchen, Dad looked up from his newspaper. "When did you get home last night?"

Really?

"None of your business," I said, picking up my pace to reach the front door.

Maybe I *should* crash on Alice's sofa until I had my own place. She'd certainly offered. But I'd been hesitant about imposing on her and her housemates.

Time to revisit that decision.

Just as my hand landed on the front door, Dad stepped right in front of me.

"You were out until three a.m.," he growled.

The depth of disgust in his already-empty eyes scared and angered me. Which should I respond to? Which would save me from a confrontation with the man?

Why did I even give a shit?

While several scenarios blazed through my mind, a flash of shame did, too, making itself at home somewhere deep inside me. I was the bad girl, the loser, the directionless daughter. The bum—as my dad had so generously called me—who was on the road selling T-shirts on the concert circuit, wasting her life.

That shame had worked a number on me. I'd allowed it to pressure me into attending nursing school.

Dad had said nursing was 'respectable.' That I'd always be 'employable.' That I'd meet the 'right' people.

He didn't say it would also be easier for him to keep an eye on me.

So I caved. I had no other idea what to do, so I figured why the hell not. And it hadn't been a bad idea, truth be told. I liked the training and so far the job was great.

And then there were the hot doctors.

"Dad. I'm twenty-five years old. Are you seriously asking me how late I stayed out?"

Irritated by my logic, he got in my face. His breath smelled like coffee. And hate.

"You're living in my house. You follow my rules."

Did he really just say that?

"I'm sorry, Dad, but this is completely inappropriate—"

His eyes narrowed. "Where were you?"

I knew better than to tell him at a party with a bunch of doctors. He'd probably fire their asses in revenge.

"Out with a couple nurse friends," I lied. "We were having fun, and closed the bars down."

Why the fuck was I telling lies? I could do whatever I wanted.

Right?

"You'd better not be lying to me," he hissed.

Okay. That was it. I'd had it.

And I knew the best weapon to hurt him with.

"You know, if Mom were here, she'd be so disappointed with you," I said.

He wasn't expecting that, and his face morphed from shock to anger. "If your mother were here, she'd be disappointed in *you*," he spat.

I held my head up and pressed my lips together so he wouldn't see them trembling. What a contradiction my life was, surrounded by so much privilege, yet overshadowed by the worst kind of tragic family bullshit.

He took a slow inhale. "Billy Quinn likes you. A lot. His parents want him to propose."

I burst out laughing.

Which was a big mistake.

"Cut it out, you little slut. You weren't out until

three a.m. with girlfriends. You have a goddamn hickey on your neck. You'd better not blow it with Billy, so help me—"

A car horn beeped out front. Thankfully, I'd told Alice to wait in the car.

As Dad peered out to see who it was, I ran out the door.

19

BOWIE

Fuck if I hadn't spent the rest of the weekend thinking about Char.

From the moment she'd walked into the party I'd had trouble taking my eyes off her. In fact, the only reason I did was that I didn't want to come off as a fucking nutcase creeper.

I saw Ace and Flynn keeping an eye on her, as well. I was glad I wasn't the only one.

The way she'd navigated a party where she really didn't know anyone, walking into the place all beautiful confidence in her tight jeans and sexy boots. She'd worn a low-cut sleeveless top that made her tits look amazing. It showed off the smooth contours of her shoulders, which I'd wanted to touch so badly I had to stuff my hands in my pockets. I'd finally had my chance on the rooftop, though, just like Ace and Flynn had.

And it was fucking hot.

She'd fallen into my kiss the same way she had back in Aspen, bewitching me and leaving me with a raging hard on. I'd been jerking myself all weekend thinking of her, and it was barely scratching my itch.

My friends and I had some… unconventional tastes. And from the first time I saw Char in Aspen, I thought she was just our flavor.

Who knew she'd reappear in all our lives?

That shit still made my head spin.

But I was beyond trying to figure it out. It had happened, and I knew not to look a gift horse in the mouth.

Kissing her, after waiting for a damn year, up on Flynn's rooftop deck, was… transcendent. Yeah, that's the way to put it.

God, I sounded like a pussy.

And when she turned to Ace just after kissing me, well I nearly blew a load in my pants.

But it was Flynn who'd taken things to the next level.

As soon as she fell into his kiss, his hands flew right to her ass, pulling her to him to grind his hard on against her.

Ace and I just looked at each other, smiling. Flynn,

the preppy silver fox with the country club background was probably the kinkiest fucker I'd ever known.

"C'mon baby," he said, leading her to a lounge chair.

He laid her back, and began to shimmy her jeans down her hips.

Her eyes widened and she sat back up, pressing her knees together. "Wait. What if someone comes up here?" She looked around frantically.

Flynn looked at us knowingly, and pulled a key out of his pocket, dangling it for all to see. "Door's locked from the outside, babe. No one can get up here. The only way we can be seen is if the neighbor's drone flies overhead, and I haven't seen it in a few days."

He looked up in the sky to check.

Char burst out laughing at that, and lay back down.

Ace and I each pulled off one of her boots, and Flynn finished with her jeans and panties to reveal a shaved and glistening pussy.

Fuck, I wanted to taste her. But it wasn't my turn.

Flynn, his gaze locked on Char's, pushed her legs open further and nodded at her.

"Hold them," he demanded.

She grabbed her legs behind her knees, opening herself for the three of us.

"Can I taste you, baby?" Flynn asked, unable to take his eyes off her pussy.

By now, Ace had her shirt pulled up and was about to remove her bra.

"Please, Flynn. Lick my pussy," she breathed.

Holy shit.

Fuck if she wasn't just as hot as I remembered in Aspen. But now I had my buddies with me, which added a level of kink I was pretty sure Char had never experienced.

Flynn ran his tongue up and down Char's pussy, causing her to squirm under him and pound her fists on the chair beneath her. He stopped for a moment to look up at Ace and me, wearing a huge grin on his wet face.

"Anybody else care to have a turn with our beautiful girl?" he asked.

I deferred to Ace, who leaned next to Char's ear.

"I want to taste you too, baby," he whispered.

She turned her head to face him, smiling and nodding, her hands flying to her now-bare breasts.

Ace took his place at the end of the lounge chair where Flynn had been, and ran a finger along her slit.

Char arched her back and sighed. "You're trying to torment me, aren't you?"

"Absolutely, beautiful."

I watched him position a finger at her opening, and slowly ease it in.

"Baby, you're tight."

I repositioned my hard cock in my jeans. I was in fucking agony.

As soon as one of Ace's fingers disappeared into Char's pussy, another one joined it. He began to pump her slowly, then picked up speed as he zeroed in on her clit with his mouth.

Flynn and I just looked at each other.

Fuck yeah.

Our girl began to convulse under Ace's ministrations, and in minutes was thrashing under him.

"Oh my god, Ace, I'm coming," she murmured between gasps.

Ace kept his tongue on her clit, prolonging her orgasm until she wriggled away, begging him to stop.

I wedged myself onto the lounge behind her, and pulled her to me while she recovered.

"Do you think there are still people downstairs?" she asked.

Flynn shrugged, laughing. "I don't really care."

20

BOWIE

There was something about Char, and it wasn't just her beauty or fucking sexiness that got me. Something in her eyes, which were hopeful and maybe tinged with a bit of sadness. She had a story.

Well, we all had stories. But I wanted to learn hers.

And I hoped she'd want to learn mine.

A group of medical residents was gathered in the cafeteria when I went to get myself a coffee.

"Holy crap. Did you see her? The new one?"

I lingered at the condiment stand, pretending to add sugar.

"She's fucking hot with that blonde hair and nice rack."

Shit.

"What's her name?"

"Not sure. Cheryl or something. But it shouldn't be hard to find out. You know, nurses are always wanting to meet doctors. That's why they become nurses to begin with."

Did someone really just say that?

"Are you going to, you know, try to talk to her?"

"I don't know. I mean, I'm sure she's conceited and all. She looks like a stuck-up bitch."

They'd just crossed the line.

I walked over to the table of four guys. I remembered when I was a medical resident. I'd been a little cocky too, until I realized how humbling saving—and losing—lives was.

"Hey, guys," I said.

They looked up at me.

"I overheard you talking about nurses, and one in particular. I don't like that."

One of them leaned back in his chair, smirking. "If you don't like it, don't eavesdrop."

I walked around the table so I could look right down on the asshole's face. "Tell me, when is your rotation in the ER?"

His face paled. I knew he hadn't expected me to be an attending physician. Ponytails and a young face do that.

He bolted upright in his seat. "Oh. Uh, I'm not sure."

"Jack, you're in the ER next month," his buddy said, laughing.

I glared at him. "Cool, Jack. I'll look forward to working with you there."

His friends snickered.

But he didn't. His eyes widened and his mouth dropped open. As I walked away from the table, nobody made a peep.

"Well, hello. If it isn't my favorite patient."

Char blushed as she took a seat on the ER exam table.

I loved that. A beautiful woman who was modest.

She was cute as hell in her green scrubs, her top neatly tucked into her drawstring pants. I looked down at my own, which were untucked, wrinkled from a cat nap I'd taken, and had a red splotch from my spaghetti lunch.

"I suppose I could have taken the sutures out myself, but it's nicer to have an expert do it," she said coyly.

I unwrapped her hand slowly, looking between it and her beautiful face. Her skin was heated and a twitch in her fingers suggested she was excited by my touch. With sterile tweezers and scissors, I started snipping the little black threads sticking out of her palm. It was a charged moment, the two of us so close and touching, but not being able to take it any further in the treatment room.

I was moving slowly. I didn't want the tension to end.

"Do you know how to take out sutures?" I asked quietly.

"Sort of. I've seen it done."

"Okay. Watch me. You pick up the thread with the tweezers until you have a little slack, and snip the thread. It should just slither out after that."

She moved for a closer look, so close I could almost kiss her temple. And I would have, had I not been at work. I took a discreet inhale of her scent, faintly perfumey and fresh, like simple drugstore shampoo.

"What if they won't come out? Like they're stuck?" She looked at me with big, earnest, eyes.

"That's when you need to soak the wound for a while."

"Good to know," she said, her gaze not wavering from mine.

Shit, I could have stared at her all day.

"Your hand healed well," I said, watching her wince as I plucked the last thread.

I still didn't believe her cut was a bagel injury, but I planned to dig into that another time. I figured if I played my cards right, there would be many opportunities to uncover her secrets.

Actually, if we guys played our cards right, we'd all

be enjoying time with this smart, confident, and sexy woman.

"Thank you for your excellent care, Doctor," she said smiling at me. "I almost want to hurt myself again so you can continue to take care of me."

There she was, my sassy girl.

I cleaned up her hand, putting a light bandage over the mostly-healed wound.

"You don't have to hurt yourself to play doctor, you know," I said.

She bit her lip.

I stepped behind the exam table to hide my stiff dick. It wouldn't do for a helpful nurse to find me in this condition.

Char and I looked at each other for an awkward moment. This was where I'd find out if she was down with us guys, or if it was a one-time thing.

Kind of like how Aspen had been.

"I'm glad you came to Flynn's party. I hope you had fun," I said, looking at her for answers.

She tilted her head. "I did enjoy it. Very much."

Fucking A.

I glanced at my watch. "Are you done for the day?"

She tried not to smile. "I am."

I peeked out of the treatment room. "I have a couple more hours. But I need a break."

I picked up a file and held it in front of my raging erection. "Go to the end of this hall and turn right. Wait for me there," I said, pointing.

Her eyes brightened, which made my dick even harder.

Jesus. What was I doing?

The logical part of my brain had stepped aside in order to let my libido take over.

Logic didn't stand a chance.

Without a word, she turned and headed out.

I headed over to the nurses' station, forcing myself to walk slowly and calmly. Of course, with the file over my cock.

"Going for a little break. You know how to reach me," I called.

"Sure thing, Doctor Grier."

It was all I could do to not break into a fucking run.

BOWIE

"C'mon," I whispered when I found Char leaning against a wall, scrolling through her phone.

We navigated a maze of hallways that left me wondering, as I often did, who the hell designed hospitals. They were worse than parking garages. I'd been at Headlands long enough to know my way around, but my first few months had consisted of constantly being lost.

When we reached our destination, I glanced up and down the hall to make sure the coast was clear. I shoved open a nondescript door, grabbed Char's hand, and pulled her into a mostly-empty storeroom I'd once taken a nap in because the on-call room had no vacant bunks.

She gasped at the sudden move, which turned me on so hard I almost forgot to lock the damn door.

Almost.

I grabbed her shoulders and pulled her to me, hungry as a madman for her sweet lips. The kiss we'd shared the other night did nothing to satisfy my craving for her. Instead, it only stoked my appetite.

I reached to the back of her neck and fumbled with a couple clips until her silky hair tumbled into my hands. I used great fistfuls of it to pull her head back, and turned her face upward toward mine. With my other hand, I ran my open palm up her neck until I had a solid grip on her chin. I turned her face slightly so I could run kisses down her temple.

She sighed. "I'm sorry I gave you a fake email in Aspen."

She ran her fingers through my hair, lightly scratching my scalp with her nails. "I was embarrassed. And I didn't know you were such a nice guy."

I laughed. "What did you think? I was an asshole?"

She laughed. "Well, I figured you were one of those guys who did stuff like that all the time. You know, pick up girls and bring them back to your room on vacation."

"So you were judging me."

She shrugged. "I guess I was. A little. I thought you

were just a man whore. So I judged you before you could judge me."

I held her chin between my thumb and forefinger. "Well, I'm judging you right now and have decided you're so fucking sexy, I can't keep my hands off you."

I checked the lock one more time and maneuvered Char over to a table. I laid her back, holding her hands above her head, with her legs dangling off the edge. Pushing between her knees, I ground against her until I could feel her pussy through my scrubs.

There was no more hiding my erection.

I untucked her top to get to her bare skin, and ran my free hand up until I reached her tits.

Fuck me.

Her nipples strained against the lace of her bra, which I pushed out of the way. I let go of her arms and pulled her breasts together, burying my face in them.

I could have licked and sucked her all day. Her tits were round and firm, and she writhed under my touch.

"Oh my god, Bowie. That feels so good," she murmured.

Well then. I was about to make her feel even better.

I kissed my way down her firm stomach until I reached the drawstring of her pants. Untying them, I pushed them to the floor where they hung off of one of her feet. She kicked and the pants flew out of our way.

She shuddered when I ran my fingers over the crotch of her panties. As I suspected, she was soaking wet.

"You good, baby?" I asked.

I looked up to see her playing with her tits.

Fuck me.

"Yeah," she whispered.

I inched aside the crotch of her panties to find her bare, glistening pussy. While I was dying to get my mouth on it, I first stroked it with my fingers, parting her puffy lips, and circling her hard clit with my thumb.

"Oh god," she murmured, her head rocking.

Well, that was all I needed.

I lowered my face between this woman's thighs and had my first taste of her beautiful pussy since Aspen. I licked and sucked until her breathing came so hard and fast that I thought I might come myself.

"Oh, oh, oh," she whispered, silently pounding her fist on the table beneath her.

She pistoned her hips against me, and when I knew she was right on her edge, I reached into my pocket for a condom.

"I want to fuck you, baby."

"Please, Bowie. Please fuck me."

I sheathed myself and slipped between her wet folds.

She drew a sharp breath, moving under me so I could fuck her better.

I reached an arm around her waist, pulling her to a seated position. I wanted to see her face while I pounded her pussy.

Her eyes fluttered opened and closed, and her head rocked from the rhythm of my pumping. She began to moan again, pushing her hand between us to rub her clit.

I put my hands under her ass and with handfuls of her flesh, pulled her to me one last time while I emptied my load.

"God, Bowie," she murmured weakly.

"You okay, baby?"

"That was even more epic than Aspen."

Goddamn right it was.

"Do you think she'll go for it?" I mused.

Ace nodded and sipped his beer. "I'm feeling good about it. I am."

He turned to Flynn who rubbed his clean-shaven chin. He took a look around the bar to make sure no one could hear us. "I think she could go either way. I'm really not sure."

It wasn't easy to find a woman who shared our particular proclivities. The three of us had been with a woman named Raffa for about a year, but in the end that didn't work out. We'd gone back to dating singly, always on the lookout for something to sate our more unconventional desires.

I knew Flynn didn't want to end up in another situation like he had with Raffa. His heart hadn't just been broken by her, but had been pretty much pulled out, stomped on, and left to bleed.

Yeah, that had not ended well.

Ace narrowed his eyes at me. "You got something going on with her, don't you?"

Fuck. Was I that transparent?

But I decided to play dumb.

He frowned, not willing to give up. "Dude, you haven't stopped smiling since we arrived. What the hell is up with you?"

I shook my head, smiling. "Guilty as charged."

"I knew it," he said, slapping the table.

Ace could read me like a book. It was something you picked up when you came from the sort of background he and I did.

Flynn, on the other hand, was sometimes blissfully unaware of what went on around him. I'd learned that those who grew up with a life of privilege like he had, were afforded safety nets. Things generally worked out okay for them. They could afford not to be on watch twenty-four-seven, looking over their shoulder for the next shit storm.

But I didn't begrudge him. I'd never do that. The man had worked hard to make his own way. In fact, on some level, I almost respected him more than someone like Ace and me. A guy like him could have taken the easy route, going after some sort of cushy career where he didn't have to work hard because he'd been born with all the money he'd ever need.

But he slogged through the journey of becoming a doctor, just like Ace and I had.

He was solid. And a good friend.

"Okay. What's next then?" I said, finishing my beer.

"We talk to her," Ace said. "See where she stands. No sense in beating around the bush. I'm taking her out for a ride on my bike tomorrow night. I'll broach the subject."

"Cool," I said. "We're counting on you, brother, to bring home our lovely girl."

22

____

CHAR

"Oh. May I help you?"

A *White Coat* had stopped by Ace's office, where I was waiting for him in the chair opposite his desk. That's what Alice and I called the doctors who walked around in white coats with their names embroidered on the front. This particular one said *Dr. Ellie Unger*.

"Uh, no, I'm fine, thank you," I said.

"Are you new?" she asked, her arms crossed as she checked me out.

I nodded. "I am. Just finished my nursing orientation."

She wasn't impressed. "Oh. You're a nurse. I heard

we were hiring more. I guess we need them." She sniffed.

Really, lady?

"What do *you* do?" I asked, even though it was obvious she was a doc. I just wanted to make her say it.

Her mouth dropped open. "I'm a *doctor*," she said, pointing at the name on her coat.

I sort of loved it when jerky people were this easy to irritate. But I did hope Ace would hurry. I didn't want to hang out with White Coat any longer than necessary.

Unfortunately for her, I was feeling salty. "Right. I mean, I know your coat says doctor, but that doesn't mean you are. Anyone can wear one of those coats. You know?"

Her face turned pink, quickly morphing to purple. She pressed her lips together, unable to come up with a response.

I settled into my seat more comfortably and started scrolling through my phone, turning it so she couldn't see the screen. I Googled her.

She looked around the office impatiently. "Um, are you here to get some orders signed or something?"

Wow. She'd gone to Harvard.

"Oh, I'm sorry. I was reading. What did you ask?" I said in my best fake sweet voice.

Ugh. What was I doing? I shouldn't be antagonizing people. I might have to work with this woman at some point. On the other hand, if I did my job competently and with a smile, no one would have a thing to complain about.

That was the thing about being a nurse. The doctors gave the orders, and we carried them out. They were dependent on us to an extent that some of them resented. It was silly, really. But if we did it well, we were superstars.

"I asked," she repeated in a slightly louder voice, "if you were here to get orders signed."

"Oh. No, I'm not here to get orders signed."

Who was this creep? And more importantly, did Ace have something going on with her? Because she seriously reminded me of a dog guarding a bone.

Not that I had any say about Ace's social life, even though he'd given me a massive orgasm on Flynn's roof deck. But he *had* invited me out for a motorcycle ride, so being on his dance card had to count for something.

And if he didn't get here soon, I had a feeling this woman might drop kick me out of his office.

Over my dead body.

I went back to my phone, but I felt her eyes firing into me. I'd clearly annoyed the shit out of her. The petty in me was satisfied.

"Well, should you *be* here?" she finally asked, tapping her foot.

God, she had nerve.

I looked up at her and smiled broadly. "Yes."

Back to the phone.

I decided to throw her a bone. "I'm so sorry I've

been remiss, but I should have asked if *you* needed something, Doctor"—I pretended to strain to read her white jacket—"Unger?"

"Hey, looks like I'm missing a party in my office!" Ace said, cheerfully bounding into the room.

"Hi, Char," he said, his spiky red hair sticking up in all directions from his surgery cap.

He was so freaking hot. And I did have a weak spot for redheads.

"Ellie, what can I do for you?" he asked, plopping down into his desk chair, leaving her nothing to do but stand.

She shifted uncomfortably. "Oh. Um. Was just saying hi."

He leaned back in his chair, hands behind his head. "Great. Thanks for stopping by. Char and I are heading out as soon as I get these scrubs off."

He looked at me with a big smile.

Dr. Unger looked confused. And unhappy. "Okay. I'll see you later."

And she took off.

"Friendly woman, isn't she?" I said.

He rolled his eyes. "I hope you didn't let her get the best of you. She's scary."

"I think I gave as good as I got." I wasn't going to say any more than that.

He stuck his head out in the hallway, looked both ways, then closed his office door.

Well.

"Hey, do you mind if I change right here? It'll be faster."

I shrugged. "Sure."

I looked out the window to pretend I wasn't checking him out. He turned his back to me and stripped off his scrubs, dropping them to the floor.

Nice.

"What kind of procedure were you just doing?" I asked, hoping my voice was steady enough to cover my nerves.

He glanced over his shoulder, his back muscles rippling as he pulled a clean, white T-shirt over his head. He stepped into some faded blue jeans and pulled on motorcycle boots. There was no way in hell anyone would think this guy was a doctor now.

And that got my heart thumping.

"I was repairing a cleft palate. We don't get a lot of those here. I like that kind of work. Makes me feel like I'm really improving someone's quality of life."

He grabbed two motorcycle helmets from the top of his file cabinet and held the door open for me.

"Do you have a jacket?"

I held up a leather one. "This seemed appropriate for a motorcycle ride."

Iris had bought it for me—with my father's money, of course—a couple Christmases ago. I'd only worn it one other time. It's not that I wasn't a leather jacket kind of girl. I was just not big on wearing things that reminded me of my stepmother.

"So where do you live? I just realized I have no idea," he said as we walked to the parking garage.

"Well, I'm living with my parents for just another month or so, and then I'll get my own place."

"Sweet," he said. "Where do they live?"

"Oh, out in the suburbs."

The less he knew, the better.

He gave me a funny look at my vague answer, but handed me my helmet, and fastened his own.

People didn't like being shut out.

They didn't like liars, either.

23

CHAR

We were out in the countryside in minutes. Ace steered us onto a quaint back road, really letting the bike rip. I held on to him tightly, my face pressed against his broad back. Every now and then I'd turn my head from one side to the other, and as I did, his leather jacket crunched against mine. He took a couple turns pretty fast, and while I squeezed my eyes closed in response, I had to say I felt damn safe.

And that felt damn good.

After about an hour, he pulled off the road, rolling the bike behind some bushes.

"What are you doing?" I asked, alarmed.

He signaled for me to climb off the back of the bike,

and then climbed off himself. "We're going for a little walk. I like to keep the bike out of sight."

Oh. Okay.

He locked our helmets and took my hand, leading the way to a cozy grove of trees with a tiny brook running through it. There, we found a picnic table basking in the last of the evening sun. We sat on top of it and watched the water trickle over and around the stones in the creek bed.

"How do you know about this place?" I asked. "It's amazing."

He looked up at the canopy of trees. "You find all sorts of cool places when you have a motorcycle. You can explore more than if you're in a car."

Ace was handsome in a different way than the other guys. Where Flynn was clean-cut and preppy, and Bowie rocked the bohemian look, Ace had a little of the wild man thing going on with his spiky hair and tattoos.

No less charming, though, especially with those green eyes and chin dimple.

I leaned back on my elbows and inhaled. What a perfect spot.

"I'd love to come back here. But I know I'll never find it on my own." I sighed

He reached for my hair, running fingers through my ponytail, which was a tangled mess from the wind. "You'll have to come back with me, then."

Was he going to kiss me? Because I sure as hell wanted him to.

Even though I'd been with Bowie just the day before.

Shit. Was all this a bad idea? Was it going to blow up in my face? Ruin my first job out of nursing school?

But I didn't care. I hadn't thought of my father or his shitty demands in a couple hours. That's what I called a good day.

"I'm glad you came with me today," Ace said.

He brought my hand to his lips and kissed the back of it just like he had on Flynn's roof.

I was glad I had my jacket on because my entire body exploded in goosebumps. No man had ever kissed my hand before him.

"Thank you for inviting me. I love motorcycles. As a passenger that is. Not as the driver."

We were silent for a moment. But not for long. I had something to get off my chest.

"You know, Ace. I was… with Bowie yesterday." I steeled myself for some sort of polite but brusque suggestion we head back home. Sure, I'd messed around with them at Flynn's party, but that was just a fluke. Right?

But he just smiled. "That's awesome."

Huh?

"Wh… what do you mean?" I asked.

He took a deep breath. "I'm glad you brought this up. I wanted to discuss it with you."

Sounded ominous.

"We guys were talking about you the other day."

They probably thought I was a huge slut.

"You were? Talking about me?"

The fresh air was suddenly a little chilled. I zipped my jacket.

"Yeah. You see, the three of us guys… like to share," he said.

Share? Share what?

I didn't have to say anything. He read my expression.

"We have… different tastes than other men. We've been known to all date the same woman. At the same time."

Was that a thing?

"And on behalf of all three of us, we wanted to let you know we'd like to get to know you better. And, you know, see where things go."

Huh.

I had questions. So many questions.

"Like you three guys and me? Together?"

He laughed, running his hand through his hair, the waning sun making his green eyes twinkle. "Just think about it. You don't have to decide anything right now."

Well.

"But I do know something," he said, turning toward me.

Was he going to say what I hoped he would?

"I really need to kiss you. Like, now."

Okay. That, I could get with.

He leaned in but stopped just short of pressing his mouth to mine. Instead, he hovered close, so close the whisper of his breath tickled my lips. If he did that to make me want him more, well, it freaking worked.

I inched closer on the picnic bench until my lips touched his. Then, as if I'd granted permission, he took my face in his hands and kissed me slowly, flicking his tongue against my lips until I parted mine and we tasted each other.

"I want to know you," he said, pulling back to look at me.

He continued to hold my face and stared, the green in his eyes interrupted by little brown flecks I'd not noticed until just then.

They were mysterious, kind of like him.

"I'm glad."

He nodded. "We're off to a good start.

24

CHAR

The ride back to the hospital was over too fast. I hated to leave Ace, who'd started telling me how he'd ended up in the military to pay for college, and about the young men he'd tried to save when he was overseas. I wanted to hear more about how he'd traveled for a year once he'd gotten out, before he'd started at Headlands.

And he'd liked my stories about being on the road, following bands, and living like a vagabond. He didn't think it was weird at all. In fact, he thought it was pretty kick-ass.

He told me I wasn't like other women he knew.

We'd hung out in that pretty grove a little too long,

oblivious to the sun's setting and the sky's turning dark. We had to fumble our way back to his bike using the light from our cell phones, holding hands and laughing as we tripped over tree roots on the way back. I normally would have been uneasy in a situation like that, but with Ace it was a great adventure.

I had him drop me at the hospital, figuring his taking me all the way home would result in nothing but a world of hurt. My dad would shit himself if he saw me with anyone, much less a doctor from the hospital. Besides, I didn't want Ace to know yet that I was related to him. He tucked my helmet in the space under his seat, and I watched him take off, listening to the roar of his bike until it faded out completely.

"Who the fuck was that?" a voice growled from behind me.

My heart jumped into my throat. The exhilaration of the ride and the warmth of connecting with Ace seeped away like it had never happened.

"Billy. Wh… what are you doing here—?"

He grabbed my good hand, interlacing his fingers with mine and squeezing until tears came to my eyes. Anyone looking might think we were just a couple holding hands, but I knew his grip was about pain and control.

"Let go of me. Now," I demanded.

I wanted to kill him. I seriously wanted this man dead.

"Get off my fucking hand," I hissed.

He took a step back, surprised by my fury. But he still didn't let me go. "Your dad sent me to get you. C'mon, we're getting out of here."

I stood my ground. "No, Billy. I'm not going anywhere with you."

So he squeezed my hand harder, the exquisite discomfort leaving me no choice but to follow him to his car to avoid a big ugly scene. My heart pounded with the terror of being at this fucker's mercy.

I could scream. Or try to run.

But I didn't.

He'd pay for this. I had no idea how, but I knew there'd be an opportunity some day.

"Don't be silly," he said, gripping my upper arm and pushing me into his car. "We're getting married. Your dad wants it. My parents want it. I want it." He held my arm for an extra few seconds to drive home his point.

He was certifiable.

He peeled into traffic with his Corvette in first gear, forcing the other cars to screech to a stop to avoid a collision. I put my hands on the dashboard to brace myself against the bouncing and squeezed my eyes closed.

"Billy, you don't even know me. We can't—"

He glanced over at me and rolled his eyes. "We can and we will. You should be glad for my offer. Your father is ruined and needs my family's money. Desperately."

Why wasn't I surprised? He and his parents were

doing nothing more than taking advantage of my dad's bad situation.

The crazy thing was, I was pretty sure Dad knew and didn't even care.

"Billy, why the hell do we have to get married for them to do business together? I don't want any part of this."

I couldn't believe I was asking such a logical question in such an illogical situation.

"God, you're so naïve," he hissed. "Must be nice to go through life without a care in the world. Our union, Char, will keep the money in the family. To put it plainly, your father can't cheat us or otherwise screw us over. And I've always wanted to fuck a girl like you. The preppy country club girls I usually meet are such boring prudes."

My hand flew to my mouth as my stomach roiled. "Billy, pull over. I'm going to be sick."

Screeching to a stop, he reached across me and pushed my door open. "Don't get anything on the car."

I leaned out and heaved until I couldn't breathe. Then the tears came. How had I ended up in such a revolting situation?

"Wh... what if I refuse to marry you?" I cried, rubbing my arm where he'd grabbed it.

It seemed he'd already considered this scenario. And wasn't too concerned by it. "Your dad will drown in his debts. He'll lose his position at the hospital like the disgraced loser that he is. Basically, he'll go down in flames. Now, you wouldn't let that happen, would you? He says you're a good daughter. That you always do what's best for the family."

Sure, as long as what's best for the family was what's best for Dad.

"And since we're getting married, I think it's okay if we start acting like husband and wife. If you know what I mean."

Oh god no.

I had to think fast. I had to get out of this car and get away from this monster.

"Um, Billy, I have an idea. I'm not feeling like myself right now. How about you take me home and we'll plan something really special, just you and me?"

His face was a mixture of suspicion and surprise at my acceptance.

So I forced a smile and took his hand.

"All right," he said.

It *was* a good idea. I just had to come up with a few others to get out of this vile situation my father had put me in.

Billy was right, I'd been a pretty dutiful daughter. Maybe not like my sister, but I'd fallen into line pretty much any time Dad had asked me to. He'd been so destroyed over my mom leaving that I'd always done just about anything I could think of to try and make him happy.

Even if it made me miserably unhappy.

25

FLYNN

I caught Bowie just as he was finishing up with a patient.

"Hey, Flynn," he said.

"Do you have a sec?" I asked.

He nodded. "Yup. Just put stitches in a kid's knee and now need to make some notes in his record. Come with me?"

We walked to the nurses' station, where there was a row of computers on a long table.

I took a seat next to Bowie and he started tapping on the keyboard.

"Hey, wanted to talk about that case you referred to Ortho yesterday."

Bowie furrowed his brow.

"You know the woman with the broken leg? From the car accident?"

Realization crossed his face. "Oh, right. Sorry, we were so swamped yesterday, and I sent three patients to Ortho." He rubbed his face over his hand, shaking his head.

The ER was a hard place to work, day after day. It could be satisfying, especially when you got a serious case, but when patients left or you referred them on, you never knew what happened to them afterwards.

I was motivated by longer-term patient relationships.

"So, how's her leg? You operate yet?" he asked.

"Well, that's what I came to talk about—oh, hey, look who we have over here," I said, gesturing toward Char on the other side of the room.

Surgical scrubs were not particularly attractive, but the way Char pulled them off was hard to ignore. Her curvy figure actually gave the shapeless garments some personality. Her hair was piled into a cute but messy confection on top of her head, and she wore a slight smudge of something shiny on her lips. That was it, no more makeup or other ornamentation.

And she was freaking perfect.

She looked our way and her face brightened. She headed straight for us.

"Gentlemen," she said, her crooked smile turning up at one corner.

"Well, if it isn't Nurse Biddle."

"Hey guys—"

"What's that on your arm?" Bowie asked, frowning and pointing at something that looked like dirt.

Char looked down at her arm, and the smile dropped from her face. "Oh. It's nothing." She tried yanking down the short sleeve of her scrub top, but it didn't help.

Then I looked more carefully and realized her upper arm had a huge bruise on it.

In the shape of a hand. A large hand.

What the hell?

"Char!" the head nurse called. "We need you over here."

Clearly grateful for the interruption, she hustled back to work, yanking her sleeve down again. She called back over her shoulder, "See you later."

Bowie and I looked at each other.

"I don't like that," he said, watching her bend to speak to an elderly patient in a wheelchair.

Her bruised arm aside, I was blown away with how gentle and kind she was with her frightened patient.

All nurses were compassionate in the beginning of their careers. Some hung on to it, but others lost it, worn down by the tireless challenges of the profession and the need to build a protective wall around their hearts. Either way, I couldn't really blame them. But I had a feeling that Char was one of the ones who'd always care. Even when it hurt her.

"She's good, isn't she?" Bowie said in a quiet voice.

In more ways than one.

"You like her, Flynn," he continued, glancing at me.

I rolled my eyes. "Of course I fucking do. You think I'm an idiot or something?"

He smiled and patted me on the back. "Ask her out then. She went riding with Ace the other day."

I wanted to. I really did. But something was holding me back. The last time we guys were in a relationship exploring our 'nontraditional' tastes, I was the one who ended up disappointed.

Actually, disappointed was an understatement. I'd fallen in love. Something I'd not planned on doing. And the woman we were in a relationship with? She didn't feel the same way. So she hit the road.

It sounded kind of pussy to say it, but I was heartbroken. Didn't need that kind of shit again.

But Bowie could read my mind. "Dude, don't hold yourself back. Char is a completely different person. Go for it."

Maybe I would.

26

FLYNN

"Thank you for joining me," I said, as Char settled into her seat opposite me.

I'd finally said *fuck it* and asked her to dinner.

She'd insisted on meeting me at a quiet little restaurant of her choosing, rather than letting me pick her up. I thought it was odd, but I figured she had her reasons, and that hopefully I'd dig into them later.

Like how the hell she came to have a hand-shaped bruise on her arm.

She settled into our table, stunning in slim jeans and a white blouse knotted at her waist. Her hair was pulled into a high ponytail, and her eyes sparkled. She slipped her phone into her purse and gazed right at me.

For a moment, I couldn't think of a single thing to say.

Which was totally fucked. I dated beautiful women all the time, most of them nurses but some were my parents' friends' daughters. They were usually part of the well-heeled country club crowd, mostly looking for wealthy husbands so they could continue their charity work, shopping sprees, and world travel on someone's dime other than their fathers'.

My parents would be thrilled if I settled down with one of these women, not because they didn't trust me to find my own partner, but for the comfort that comes in pairing off with someone from the 'same world' we lived in, as they put it.

Their elitism disgusted me, but I tried to hold compassion for them. They didn't know any better, and people were usually afraid of what they didn't know.

"Wine?" I finally managed, holding the bottle up for her to inspect.

She didn't even look at it, just kept her gaze on me. Christ, how many women had I known who had to check out my selection before they decided whether or not it was good enough for them.

"Please. I'm dying for some," she said.

As soon as I poured, she held her glass up. "Cheers," she said with a brilliant smile.

"Cheers. And welcome to Headlands Hospital. May it and nursing be the calling of your dreams."

She frowned momentarily, then righted her face.

"What? You don't like it already?" I asked.

She furrowed her brow as she thought. "I do like it. At least I think I do."

She leaned closer, as if she were telling me a secret. "I'd never particularly wanted to be a nurse. I kind of just fell into it."

Okay. I'd never heard that before.

I was suspicious. "Studying nursing is a lot of work. I don't see how you kind of just 'fall into it.' It seems like it takes a lot of commitment to get through."

She nodded. "Of course, of course. It's just that… I was kind of aimless, and my dad suggested it, so I said why not."

Was it too soon to reach for her hand?

Fuck, dude. Calm yourself.

"So how'd *you* get into medicine, Doctor Morrow?"

Ah, the question every doctor got, over and over and over. Most answered it with the insipid 'I wanted to help people' because it was the easy answer and discouraged follow-up questions. But the reasons people went into medicine were far more complex than that.

Like my reasons were.

I wasn't about to dump the 'I wanted to help people' spiel on Char. No, I was going to be real with her. If wanted the same in return, how could I expect it if I didn't lead the way?

"I had a brother two years older who was going into

medicine. Like a lot of little brothers, I did pretty much everything he did."

She just kept looking at me. She knew there was more to it.

And she was right.

"He's gone now. My brother."

Her eyebrows rose. "Gone? As in deceased?"

I nodded and took a swig of my wine.

She reached for my free hand. "What happened?"

Would I ever get used to telling this story?

I already knew the answer to that.

"I was finishing up medical school, and he was in his residency. We were out one night and got in a car accident. A bad car accident. I made it, he didn't. I was the one driving."

I'd spilled the story as fast as I could. Figured it would be easier that way.

Her eyes widened the way everyone's did when they heard what happened, but hers weren't full of pity. She saw my pain and I could swear it was as though she were willing to shoulder some of it with me.

She shook her head slowly. "I'm sorry."

I pulled my hand from hers like the fucking idiot that I was, and looked straight down at my menu, even though I already knew what I wanted. When I'd gathered myself, I looked back up at her.

"Thank you."

The waiter came by. Char asked a few questions and then ordered. I did the same.

"Now that I've been straight with you, will you be straight with me?" I asked.

Her eyes widened and she pulled her arms closer to herself. "What do you mean?" she asked, discomfort flooding her eyes.

"I want to know about the bruise on your arm."

She hesitated for a moment, then recovered. "Oh that. Well, that's just a misunderstanding I had with a… family friend."

Her gaze was steady, giving nothing away.

Fuck all. If she wasn't going to talk, then I'd just have to wait until she trusted me more.

But I stared right back at her, making it clear I knew she was lying.

27

CHAR

"Oh my god, that was delish. I just love this little place. It's so… private."

And private was what I desperately craved. I couldn't have Billy or anybody else see me out and about until I found a solution to my predicament.

Yeah, like I would marry that fucker. His parents, my parents, and he were total loons.

How did this shitshow get so out of control? I mean, in what world do dads tell their daughters who to marry?

Not my world.

Then why did I let things go this far? Why didn't I

tell them all to go to hell, and just walk out? Crash at Alice's until I could get my own place?

Christ, there was even a bulletin board at work where nurses were looking for roommates.

I was an idiot. And disgusted with myself.

And I knew perfectly well why I'd reacted the way I had. Or *not* reacted, if I were to be accurate.

When my mom bailed, I was six and Franny eight. It nearly destroyed my dad. He still went to work every day, but at night when he came home, he barely said hello, and just went to his bedroom and shut the door.

That's when my sister and I started cooking. It didn't take us long to realize if we didn't figure out how to feed ourselves, we'd starve.

We also tried to feed Dad, who was inconsolable. He could barely speak, just staring at the walls of his room for hours on end. Franny and I were terrified. But she was smart and figured shit out. We found YouTube videos on doing the laundry and making our favorite dishes.

We were pretty proud of ourselves.

But we were also tormented by Dad's suffering, and that torment had followed us the rest of our lives. We tiptoed around the man, doing everything we could to protect him from any further hurt.

We were so occupied with helping him survive, we barely took time to realize what Mom's leaving meant to *us*.

He'd told us plain and simple that she didn't love

any of us anymore. She was gone forever, he'd said. We believed him.

What choice did we have?

We cried, but with only one parent left, we turned our focus on him.

It was amazing how people could have a hold over you, even when it no longer made sense.

"Would you like to come home with me?" Flynn asked, a shock of silver hair falling on his perfectly sculpted forehead. He pushed it back absentmindedly, his intense gaze bringing me almost to the point of discomfort.

Almost.

"I'd love to," I said.

I'd figure out how to get home later. And what I'd do when I got there.

All I knew was I wanted to spend more time with this sexy, smart, heartbroken man. The weight of blaming himself for his brother's death must have been infinite, as was the pain he lived with.

I wasn't clear on why the guys didn't mind each other hanging out with me. I guess it was just their kink. I wasn't complaining. Three smart, fine-looking men liked me and wanted to get to know me. It was like winning the man jackpot.

"Your apartment is so cool," I told him when we arrived.

Of course, I'd told him that the previous time I'd

been there, during his party, but it was worth repeat-
ing. Because his place *was* fucking awesome.

"Thank you. I feel like I should tell you that it was
basically a gift from my parents for finishing medical
school."

I turned to look at him. I didn't care how he
acquired his place, but I liked that he wanted to be
honest with me.

I supposed he wanted me to be honest with
him, too.

"Can we go up on the roof deck again?" I asked. "It
was so pretty up there."

Flynn handed me two wine glasses, grabbed a bottle
of white from the fridge, and led the way.

I'd been a little distracted when I'd last been there,
getting down and dirty with the three guys, so now I
took the opportunity to look around. The deck was
more beautiful than I even remembered. Lit by hidden
spotlights, it had several different seating areas with
outdoor sofas and lounge chairs, and was dotted with
raised planters holding an assortment of succulents
and wild grasses. It was like a mini resort.

Flynn and I took seats next to each other, and he
poured us each some wine. I sat with my head tilted
back on the wicker sofa, and looked at the stars visible
in the night sky.

"This is so relaxing. You must love coming up here
after a long day at work."

His fingers reached for mine, entwining them

loosely. "You have no idea. This is my sanctuary. Sometimes I come up here to chill for a bit. Then I conk out and wake up in the middle of the night, wondering where I am."

I turned to run my fingers through his thick, silvery hair.

"Does everyone in your family go prematurely gray?" I asked, lightly rubbing his scalp with my fingernails.

He closed his eyes at the sensation. "Just the men. Who knows about my mom—she could be gray, but she colors her hair. When my brother died, he was almost completely gray."

"Your hair is so thick," I said, continuing with my finger combing.

"Mmmm. That feels good."

"I think I've turned you into a big pile of mush," I laughed.

His eyes flew open, and he nodded. "You have. And now it's my turn to do the same to you."

He laid me back on the sofa, nudging my knees apart with his until he was between my legs. Holding himself up with his arms, he leaned over me, his lips hovering just above mine. As he had all evening, his gaze drilled into mine, intense and demanding. But somehow, this time, I didn't find it as intimidating.

I reached up, placing my hands on either side of his handsome face, and brought him closer until our lips met.

At first his mouth was light on mine—not much more than a breathy whisper of a kiss, so controlled it was out of control.

We weren't really even doing anything yet, and I was already breathing hard in anticipation. I was hungry for his affection, so damn hungry. The past few days had been difficult. I wanted to forget everything, and just feel for a while, feel everything he could make me feel.

And as I wished for more, it was like he read my mind. Or maybe my body gave me away. Flynn pressed his lips hard against mine in a delicious fury that connected our pain and joy in a way I didn't think I'd ever experienced.

As his lips and tongue explored mine, his erection ground against my sex, the hard denim of our blue jeans making our grinding deliciously agonizing.

I grabbed for the buttons of my blouse and tore at them, dying to feel him against my bare skin. I wriggled out of it, unhooked my bra, and threw both aside. His eyes traveled over me the way they had the night I'd been with him and the guys, but tonight he was taking his time, savoring every bit of me and our time together.

His own breath deepened as his mouth found my nipple, taking my sensitive flesh between his teeth and rolling it nearly to the point of pain. He stopped only when I began to moan.

"You're so hot, baby," he murmured, grinding his hard cock against me.

"Do you have a condom, Flynn?" I asked.

"Yeah," he said, studying me again.

God, he was intense.

He climbed off me, producing a small packet from one of his pockets. He pulled his T-shirt off and unbuckled his pants, pushing them and his boxers to the ground. He kicked everything aside in a pile, and stood before me, his cock the only thing more rock hard than his muscular, defined body.

He ran his hand up and down his long, thick shaft in a movement so hot I groaned. Would I be able to handle him?

But before I could spend too much time thinking, he unbuttoned and shimmied my jeans down to my feet, pulling off my boots and socks first.

"You're beautiful," he said in a thick voice.

He rolled the condom on and positioned himself over me where he'd been moments before, separated from me by our jeans.

He reached between my legs, and finding my soaked pussy, ran his fingers through my puffy folds, parting my lips to reach my most private parts. His cock touched against my opening, and he stopped before going any further.

"Are you ready, baby?"

I nodded. "Yeah. I am. Please fuck me," I whispered.

That was all the invitation he needed. He plunged

inside me up to his balls, groaning and grinding himself deeper.

"God you feel good, it's so good," he murmured, sliding in and out.

The vibration building in my core spread to my limbs. When it reached my throat, it turned into a growing hum that left me panting and thrashing until an orgasm plowed through me.

"Flynn, Flynn, I'm coming now," I cried.

He groaned, driving inside me to his balls and holding himself there, his cock throbbing until he joined me, coming in a pulsating rhythm.

"Holy shit," he said, laughing. "I think this nurse is trying to kill me."

28

CHAR

Shit.

Shit, shit, shit.

It was six a.m. Flynn and I had fallen asleep after moving inside and settling in his bed to watch a movie.

I jumped up and started yanking my clothes on.

He opened his eyes, squinting in the morning sun. "Hey, let me give you a ride home."

Oh shit. That again.

"No thanks," I said, pulling my shoes on. "I'll call an Uber."

He frowned. "What the fuck, Char? Who do you live with? Are you married?"

"No, of course not. It's just that I'm staying at my

dad's for a bit. I can't have him see you dropping me off."

That seemed to satisfy him. At least for the time being.

I leaned onto the bed and kissed his cheek. "I gotta run. I'll see you later at the hospital. Thank you for an amazing night." I kissed him once more and took off.

♥

"Nurse Biddle, the patient in treatment room four is ready for an IV," Rosso said, with a dismissive wave of her hand.

What a gal.

I checked the doctor's orders for the patient and gathered everything I needed. I wheeled it into the room on a tray and smiled weakly.

"Hello, Mr. Bourke," I said, trying to disguise my panic at starting this elderly man's treatment.

The problem was, I couldn't do this alone. There was no fucking way. I poked my head out of the curtain, but there were no other nurses in sight. Except Rosso. I'd die before I'd ask her for assistance.

Dammit.

"Hey, Char, what are you up to?"

Ohthankgod.

"Bowie," I whispered, glancing back over my shoulder to make sure Mr. Bourke couldn't hear me. "I have to do an IV. By myself."

He whispered back. "Can you do it? Do you know how?"

"I think so. But I don't want to do it alone. It's my first one outside of school."

He patted my arm and glanced over at Rosso. "Jesus. You'd think she could help one of her new staff. But I'll try and help you. I don't do this very often, but between the two of us I think we can get the patient set up."

"Oh my god, Bowie, thank you."

Doctors almost never did this kind of grunt work. I knew he wouldn't be adept at it, but at least he could guide me. Hopefully.

I smiled at my patient. "Mr. Bourke, Doctor Grier and I are going to put in your IV."

"Okay," he murmured, the pure vulnerability in his voice scaring the shit out of me.

What if I fucked up?

"Okay, let's start here," Bowie said, looking at the patient's orders.

He threaded the lines together just like they'd shown us in school. "What do you think?" he asked.

I wracked my memory and had to say, it looked pretty solid.

"Great. Now let's add the saline and everything else."

Bowie leaned close to the old man's ear. "You got a good one, Mr. Bourke. She's our best nurse."

I almost melted all over the floor. I loved how he handled patients.

And I love the way he handled me.

He winked and took off.

Mr. Bourke's eyes widened, and he smiled, patting my arm with his withered hand. I just wanted to kiss him.

Victory. Not only had I not killed anyone, I actually got my patient to smile.

But just as I left the treatment room, Nurse Rosso appeared. Where was she when I needed her?

"Why was Doctor Grier helping you? Don't you know how to set up an IV?" she snapped.

Bowie was standing not far away, updating patient notes on a computer. He glanced at Rosso, looked back at me, and rolled his eyes with a smirk.

I held my head up. Bowie and I had done a good job together. Hospitals were all about teamwork… supposedly. "He offered to help me, and I gratefully accepted."

She narrowed her eyes, pissed I hadn't bowed to her authority. "Doctor Grier has better things to do than help you. You just wasted his valuable time."

She glanced over at Bowie, expecting him to concur. But he just frowned at her.

And that pissed her off more.

She looked at the clock. "Can you come to my office with me?" Turning on her heel, she started walking, certain that I'd follow.

And I did.

What a pain in the ass she was. But I reached for my mantra of *compassion*. Word had it she had nothing else going on in her life but work. So I had to let her have that.

"Please have a seat," she said, gesturing to the lone chair opposite her desk.

I squeezed into the tight space she'd managed to stuff a straight-back wooden chair into, sitting with my legs diagonal for lack of space. No one could sit there comfortably, but Rosso had undoubtedly added the chair on the pretense of having lots of important meetings.

Nurses rarely got offices, but because Rosso had, she clearly wanted everyone to know. She'd gotten a huge sign with her name on it for her door, and even had her 'office room number' in her email signature and on her business cards.

Never missed a chance to impress, that one.

She folded her hands and looked at me benevolently. Which meant she was going to be anything but benevolent.

"You know, Char, Doctor Grier is a very friendly man."

If she only knew.

"In fact, he and I were an item for a short time."

Oh, for Christ's sake.

Bullshit alert.

"But I'm with a much better man now," she said with satisfaction.

It took me a moment to realize she was waiting for me to acknowledge her relationship prowess. So I did.

"That's wonderful. It really is."

She smiled and sat back in her chair, satisfied by my nod to her good life choices.

Which made me realize that since she was so easy to flatter, I might do a little further kissing up while I had the opportunity.

I wasn't above that sort of thing.

"Thank you for reminding me the doctor's time is very valuable."

I nearly choked on the words.

But Rosso smiled like she'd just won the damn lottery.

29

ACE

The bastard.

"As you know, Ace, there are concerns among the hospital leadership team about your past."

I usually admired the faces of the aged, with their lines and crevices portraying all they'd seen and lived.

But on Doctor Cole, all I could see was ugly betrayal in his sunken eyes and papery yellow skin that looked as if you were to touch it, it would fall right off.

And that's how I felt about him overall, at that moment. He, a man of immeasurable privilege, was giving me shit about my long-ago troubled childhood. How anyone could judge someone for having been born on the wrong side of opportunity was beyond me.

Never mind I served in the fucking US Army and put back together boys that his generation thought were expendable.

I certainly wasn't going to share with him that I had a brother in prison.

The old fucker. He wasn't even that good at what he did, which I believed lowered the level of care our patients got. But he was buddies with some of the folks on the board of directors, not to mention the hospital CEO, Charles Biddle.

I took a deep breath to calm myself and ensure I spoke only in the most civil of tones. It wouldn't pay to let him know how I felt about him, his skills as a plastic surgeon, or his elitist perspective.

"Thank you for letting me know that, Doctor Cole. I can assure you, my past is just that, and I am committed to providing the best care possible to patients here at Headlands."

He sat back in his chair, suspicious of being patronized—that's how cynical a jerk he was.

Really, there was nothing I could say that would satisfy him.

"Well, Ace, I wish it were all as simple as that."

Jesus. He was doubling down.

"If it gets out that we have a former juvenile delinquent on our physician team, well, that wouldn't look very good for Headlands. Now would it?" He looked at me like he'd just explained something to a toddler.

"Not sure I agree with that, sir—"

But he waved away my response. "You might want to think of other options, Ace."

What the fucking fuck. Did he really just say that? He couldn't even hold a scalpel steady anymore.

I pressed my lips together so I didn't say something I might regret and pushed myself to my feet. "I'll let you know what I decide, Doctor Cole. I do have one more year in my contract you know."

He nodded smugly. "I know that."

Working at County was looking better every day.

"Oh, Ace, one more thing."

I stopped in the doorway and turned. This fucker might have power over me now, but he wouldn't for long.

"If you're interested in working on the paper the department is putting together for publication, we could use the help. You might even get your name on it."

Generous of them.

My response took every ounce of restraint I had. "I'll let you know."

Yeah right. *Cold day in fucking hell*, and all that.

I was wound into such a tight bundle of rage that I nearly wiped someone out when I hurled the stairwell door open.

I'd definitely be working off steam with a few hours on my bike later.

Until then, I took several deep breaths. I was heading to see a patient and needed to be on point.

But when I walked into my patient's room, I stopped short. Who was before me but the lovely Char, who was teaching another nurse how to set up an IV.

"Oh, hello, Doctor," Char said with a twinkle. "We're just about finished up here."

She turned to her fellow nurse. "Does that seem pretty clear, how it all gets set up?"

Her coworker looked at her gratefully. "Thank you so much. Really."

"Of course. Someone was nice enough to teach me, so I'm happy to teach you. Just pay it forward."

"Good job," I said to them as they left, wondering if Char were free for a ride that evening.

Just when I was about to start talking to my patient, Nurse Rosso appeared in the doorway. "Doctor, could I have a moment with you?"

I excused myself.

She looked at me with her permanently pained expression.

"What can I do for you, Giovanna?" I asked.

She cleared her throat, thrown off by being addressed by her first name. "Doctor Hardin, I saw you watching those new nurses. Tell me, were they doing something incorrectly? I need to know things like that.

Don't worry, you won't get them in trouble. I need to ensure the floating nurses are one of the strongest groups in the hospital. They see such a multitude of cases, moving from department to department."

Was she serious? Spying on her staff and expecting doctors to rat them out? God, she was horrible.

"Giovanna, they did nothing wrong. In fact, I was admiring how they were working together so well."

She looked surprised.

"Can I ask you a question?" I said, moving closer to her.

She nodded with enthusiasm, tilting her head to hear me and clearly still hoping I'd tell her something that would give her cause to scold someone. Maybe even take somebody down.

"Do you want to see your team fail, Giovanna? Because it seems like it."

Her eyes bulged, and she pressed her lips together until they turned white. "Wha… what are you talking about? That's ridiculous."

Her mouth opened as if she were going to protest further, but snapping it closed, she stormed away, her heavy wooden clogs echoing down the hallway.

First chance I got, I called my brother. Well, I didn't exactly call him directly. The way it worked in prison was I had to leave a message for him, and he called if and when he got it, and if and when he were permitted.

So, in short, the chances of my hearing back from

him after leaving a message were probably fifty-fifty at best.

But this time I got lucky.

"Dillon," I said, after I'd accepted his return, collect call.

"Hey, little bro. Everything good?" he asked.

He knew something was up. We rarely spoke more than once a month, and I'd just been on the phone with him the week before.

I couldn't lie. It felt good to hear his voice. The man might have been a convicted felon serving his time, but he was my big brother, and had always taken his duty to watch over me seriously. He couldn't do much from prison except listen, which was exactly what I wanted just then.

I told him the story of Cole essentially putting the screws to me about my brief but successful bout as a juvenile delinquent.

"No shit," Dillon said. "He's giving you a hard time for being a punk when you were fifteen? God, what an ass. Hey, how'd they find out anyway?"

"Well, I don't exactly hide it. I mean, when I talk to school kids, I'm always open with my story to show them how I turned myself around. And now that fucker is holding it against me. I tell ya, Dil, poverty is the gift that keeps on giving. Just when I think I've risen above our shitty circumstances, something comes along to try and push me right back into them."

"You've done remarkable things Ace. You don't need me to tell you that, but shit, look at me. You could have ended up right where I am. But you used your goddamn head and made better decisions. I'm proud of you, little bro. No one's surprised I ended up in prison, but I sure as hell bet people from the old neighborhood would be surprised you're a fucking doctor."

My voice caught in my throat, and for a moment, I thought I might actually shed a tear. There wasn't a goddamn thing about life that was fair. Opportunities might or might not come your way. If they did, fine—you became a doctor. If they didn't—you ended up in prison. The opposite ends of chance.

"So, what are you going to do?" he asked.

I'd only played around thinking of the possibilities. Maybe now was the time to get serious.

"I talked to someone I know at County Hospital, a former professor of mine. It might be a good fit. I have one more year in my contract here, although I could probably break it if I needed to."

"You'll know when it's the right time to make a move," Dillon said.

I hesitated before continuing.

Oh, what the fuck.

"Dil, I've met this woman. She's a nurse here."

He whistled quietly. "Jesus. I haven't heard you talk about a woman in a long time, dude."

I laughed. He was right. I didn't usually talk about

the women I dated. But there was something about Char…

"She's amazing, Dil. I mean, she's beautiful, sure, but she's also smart and cool. Down to earth."

What was I talking about? I barely knew her. But I wanted to know her better, that was for damn sure.

30

CHAR

"How'd you get a name like Charleigh, anyway?"

I glanced around Flynn's ultra-modern loft where I'd been just a couple days before. It was here that I could really breathe for the first time in ages. His place felt like a fortress. A big, safe fortress.

And safe was what I needed. Desperately.

"You're not going to believe it if I tell you."

Ace and Bowie looked at each other, their brows furrowed.

"Well, now you have to tell us," Ace said, shaking his head.

Sitting opposite these two beautiful men while Flynn banged around in his kitchen preparing us steaks and salad, I felt a familiar twitch between my legs, which crawled up to my belly, leaving me shifting uncomfortably in my tight blue jeans.

How did they do that, dammit?

And now they were going to learn one of my most shameful secrets.

I took a deep breath. "My father's name is Charles. If I'd been a son, I would have been Charles, Junior. So Charleigh was his next best."

I could see the wheels turning as they put it all together.

Charles Biddle…. It was as if the words were hanging in the air.

Bowie opened his mouth to ask the question I'd known was coming.

But I cut him off. "Further, my sister is named Franny, short for Frances, because my dad's middle name is Francis."

Yeah, he was a vain asshole.

I took a sip of the expensive wine Flynn had just opened.

Ace leaned forward in his chair, his expression pained. "So… your father is Charles Biddle? The CEO of Headlands Hospital? Where we all work?"

Flynn emerged from the kitchen, a chopping knife in one hand and a green pepper in the other.

And the three guys looked at me like I had two heads.

It was to be expected.

"He is." I looked directly at Bowie. "I didn't want you to know when you first asked. So, when you were giving me my stitches, I lied. I'm sorry."

He nodded slowly, his gaze not budging from mine, taking in the news.

"Holy fuck," Flynn burst out.

Ace just rubbed his hand over his face like he was tired.

"I knew I couldn't keep this from you forever. It seemed as good a time to fess up as any. I hope I didn't ruin the evening."

It was clear I had.

Shit.

After a few more moments of silence, I stood. "I think I'm making everyone uncomfortable. I'll leave now." I cleared my throat so no one would hear my voice crack.

Fuck.

"Hold on!" Ace called, jumping to his feet. He crossed the room in huge strides and took both my hands in his.

"You're not going anywhere. Yeah, it's a hell of a shock to find out you're Biddle's daughter, but that doesn't change how we see you."

He pulled me down on the sofa next to him and put an arm around my shoulder. "Why did you keep this from us?"

Ugh. Where to begin.

I decided to keep it simple.

"Because he's a horrible man. I'm ashamed of him. I'm ashamed of being related to him. And... I'm living at his house now. But it's just a temporary arrangement."

There. I'd done it. Completely and totally humiliated the shit out of myself.

My dishonesty should have come as no surprise. The guys weren't fans of Dad's. In fact, I think the only people at Headlands who were, were the old timers he'd snowed over with his charm.

That was a shitty excuse, though.

"Is that why you wouldn't let me drop you home?" Flynn asked.

I nodded. I was such an idiot.

It had been kind of Ace to assure me they weren't upset at my deception, but after they had some time to think about it, I had no doubt they'd be done with me. No one would want to be involved with the daughter of such a dreadful man. Further, they'd be putting themselves right in harm's way should my dad find out about our... relationship.

Or whatever you called it.

I looked down at my hands where I was wringing them in my lap. I wanted to be tougher and let them know I could care less whether they stuck around. But there was no disguising my feelings on this one.

The shame was real.

What the hell had I thought would come of this thing I had with the guys? It could never go anywhere.

Dad was forcing my hand, and he'd have me walking down the aisle with Billy in no time unless I could find some way out.

I debated for a moment sharing the whole, sordid story with the guys, but there was no way I could drag them into my drama. It was bad enough my dad was willing to ruin my life without impunity. What he'd do to them could be far worse.

"Char, are you listening?" Ace asked, turning my face up to his.

Bowie and Flynn were staring at me intently, too.

I shook my head. "Sorry. Lost in thought."

I wished I could get lost in more than that.

"Baby, we're not going anywhere," he said.

Bowie nodded. "Yeah, Char. You think we'd bail over that? You are not your dad."

"You guys have no idea—"

"Hold on," Flynn said, holding his hands up, "we have something to discuss with you before you go any further."

I laughed. "I can just imagine. Does it start with *get the hell out of my house?*"

It wasn't funny, really, but something needed to break the tension.

"What we want to say," Bowie started, "is that we all want to be with you. Like in a relationship with you."

I looked at Ace. He hadn't been kidding when he'd mentioned 'sharing.'

"It's unusual. We'll be the first to admit it," Bowie said.

He looked at the other two guys, who nodded in unison.

"But it's our thing. We *share*."

At that moment I both hated and loved my life.

How fucked was that?

"You share… *women*. That's what you're getting at, right?"

Ace hadn't been kidding.

Flynn continued. "We've done it before. It's fucking awesome. Intimate, taboo, and incredibly erotic."

I wasn't sure I understood, but the way they were looking at me with such desire sent a zipping wave of need through me.

I wanted to be kissed. Right then, right there.

Because Ace was closest, I pulled him to me. His lips brushed over mine, and I don't know how, but I could feel him telling me everything would be okay.

I pulled back and looked at Flynn and Bowie. Their eyes said the same.

I stood and began to unbutton my blouse. Then, I kicked off my shoes and peeled down my jeans. I stood before three beautiful men in nothing but a lace bra and matching panties.

Bowie immediately stroked me between my legs. "You're wet, baby. All the way through your panties." He gazed at me with a wicked grin and pressed his hand against my heated core.

"Mmmm. You smell so fucking good," Ace murmured from behind me, pushing my long hair aside, his lips passing over the back of my neck.

I was sinking. Or was it flying? It didn't matter—all that did was that I was no longer preoccupied with the ugliness in my life. I let my eyes flutter closed as three pairs of hands helped themselves to my body. Which I was happily giving to them.

Someone removed my bra and panties. I thought to open my eyes and see who, but what did it matter?

Thick fingers stroked my pussy, entering my folds and humming over my clit. Tremors sped throughout, and I grabbed the shoulders of whoever was closest in order to remain upright.

Arms wrapped around me from behind, finding my breasts and twisting my nipples.

Someone's hand took mine and rubbed it over blue jeans containing a huge erection. I unzipped the fly that was in my way and pushed through a tangle of fabric until I touched hot flesh and a drop of precum.

I stroked the cock down to its balls, where I fingered them lightly, and then back up to its bulbous head.

The arms behind me left my breasts and grabbed fistfuls of my ass, kneading it and spreading me apart. Someone was looking at me back there, and I was loving it. I wanted the guys to see all of me. Everything about me.

A finger slipped inside my pussy, my walls clamping

down on it hungrily. I opened my eyes and moaned into Flynn's mouth.

Bowie was next to me, moving his hips in and out of my grip as I stroked his fat cock.

"Sit," he demanded.

Flynn's finger slipped out of me, and Ace's hands released my ass. As I sat on the edge of the sofa, Bowie brought his cock to me, stopping at my lips and rubbing over them like a balm.

I wanted to taste him so badly I grabbed his length and directed it right into my mouth, not stopping until he banged the back of my throat. I choked lightly, and he groaned, clearly pleased with my efforts.

"Oh yeah. Suck my cock, baby," he murmured, rocking his hips against my face.

Flynn and Ace took seats next to me, one of them playing with my breasts and the other stroking my clit. I rocked myself against their hands while pistoning Bowie. I was one big ball of sensation and was where I wanted—and needed—to be at that moment.

"Should I keep going, baby?" Bowie growled. "Can you handle my cum?"

"Mmmm…" I mumbled, nodding.

Flynn slipped two fingers inside me and began to pump while Ace pinched and played with my nipples.

"Oh fuck!" Bowie groaned, thrusting to the back of my throat and holding himself there.

I swallowed as fast as I could, and when I couldn't

take anymore, pulled him out of my mouth, directing his semen onto my breasts.

"Fucking hot," Ace said, smiling ear to ear as Bowie shot his load all over me.

I was a mess. My hair was a tangled mop, I knew I had mascara running down my cheeks, and I was trembling. Flynn drove his fingers deep inside me, in and out, until my head dropped back and I let out a scream.

"Yeah," I moaned with pleasure, Flynn fucking me into oblivion with his fingers.

When I stopped shaking, the guys lowered me on the sofa. Flynn brought a wet cloth and started to wipe me down.

"Oh my god, that was so fucking hot," I mumbled. "I want more."

"Don't worry, baby. There's plenty more," one of them assured me.

31

CHAR

I looked around the bedroom I'd taken in my dad's house, trying to assess what I could cram in a couple duffle bags. I had to get the fuck out. There was no longer any question.

"Alice," I said quietly on my cell.

"Char? Why are you whispering? What's wrong?"

I stuck my head in the hallway to see where Dad and Iris were. No big surprise, their voices wafted up from the kitchen where they were bickering.

"Does the offer still stand to crash at your place?" I asked.

"Of course it does. Why? What's wrong?"

I had so much to tell her.

"Come get me at nine p.m. Can you do that?"

"Sure. No problem. See you then."

I gathered the basics of what I needed and crammed it into my bags. Packing too much stuff would draw attention, and I figured anything I forgot, I could just buy.

Thank god I could wear scrubs at work.

Then, I tucked the bags into my closet to keep them out of view.

The front doorbell rang. I smoothed out the knee length dress Iris had gotten me and slipped on some simple flats. She was going to love my outfit, which would make Dad happy, too. The more compliant I was with their tastes, the less they'd suspect I was up to something.

"Hello, Mrs. Quinn," I said, extending my hand.

She looked me up and down. "You look very nice, Char."

She never complimented me.

"Isn't that dress darling on her?" Iris asked, running to air kiss our guest. "I picked that up for her at Saks. I knew it would be beautiful on her."

"Char, honey," Mr. Quinn said, giving me a big bear hug.

And then there was Billy. All eyes were on us as we greeted each other.

Might as well fucking go for it. I gave him a smile.

"Hey, baby," he said with his smarmy grin.

Baby?

I threw my arms around him anyway, like he was my long-lost love, realizing exactly how short he was after having been with the guys.

When we released each other, I took his hand like we were a real couple.

I think everyone was surprised, but no one more than I. It was killing me, this phony affection, but it was necessary.

"Shall we have drinks?" Iris asked, clapping in delight.

Dad, Mr. Quinn, and Billy had scotch. Without asking us, we ladies were served white wine.

Interesting.

Everyone chitchatted politely with the exception of Dad, who, when the conversation steered away from him or his prospective radiology business, spoke a little louder until everyone looked his way and waited for him to finish.

Probably as tired of Dad's blustering as I was, Billy steered me to a corner of the library on the pretense of looking at one of the huge books I was sure no one in the house had ever opened, much less read.

"How're you doing, baby?" he asked, kissing my temple.

Ugh.

But I smiled brightly. "Great," I squeaked.

He tilted his head, nodding. "I have a surprise for you." He looked me up and down.

Oh shit. Not that.

Definitely not that. I wasn't sure how to let him know my dress was not coming off, at least not in his company.

My dad and Mr. Quinn tapped the side of their glasses to call everyone to attention. Mrs. Quinn and Iris beamed.

What were they so fucking happy about?

They all nodded at Billy.

Was *this* my surprise?

He dropped to one knee.

Oh no. Please god no.

The parents gathered around.

"Char, I know you've been waiting for this moment..."

This is what I got for playing nice.

"...and the time is finally here. I discussed this with your dad, and he's fully on board."

He took a little box out of his pocket.

And just as he started to open it, I grabbed him by the arm and pulled him to his feet. "Get up, Billy. Get up for Christ's sake."

To prove how completely dense the guy was, he continued smiling. He extended the box in my direction again, obviously expecting me to happily accept it.

So I smacked his hand, and the box went flying. The smile faded from his face, replaced with confusion.

He turned to look at his parents, like a hurt puppy.

Oh. My. God.

How did I get mixed up with such a bunch of losers?

My dad took a step toward me. "Now Char, dear—"

"Don't touch me!"

As I dashed across the room, Dad grabbed my arm. But I yanked it free and ran to my room, two steps at a time with him hollering after me.

I slammed my bedroom door and locked it. "Alice? Come get me now. Please," I begged her, shaking so hard I could hardly hold the phone.

"Okay. I'll be there in fifteen. I'll call when I'm out front."

I heard some goodbyes and the front door slammed shut. The house became dead quiet.

Awesome. The Quinns had bailed.

I wanted to text the guys so badly. They'd know just what to do, and what to say.

But it would also be selfish. They'd be over here in a flash to help, and that would be the end of their medical careers. Even if they left Headlands, my father's retaliation would be vicious and unrelenting. He'd been in the business of medicine for a long time, and his tentacles stretched far.

But I had a plan. I'd get to Alice's and then let the guys know where I was. I wasn't sure I understood their 'relationship' offer, or if I would actually take them up on it, but their friendship meant everything. I knew they'd never take that away.

My phone buzzed with a text.

i'm here

be down in five, I responded.

I couldn't believe I was escaping from my dad's house, but that's what it had come down to. I stuffed a few more things in my bags and slung one over each shoulder. I slipped out of my room on tiptoes, hoping Dad and Iris were busy arguing, like they usually were.

I hustled down the stairs and straight for the front door when Dad and Iris opened it and walked inside, stopping right in front of me.

What were they doing outside?

"Char, we already sent Alice home. Told her you were not well."

What?

I yanked the front door open and saw her headlights disappear into the street.

"Why?" I cried. "Why are you doing this?"

Dad yanked my bags from me and started walking back upstairs with them.

"Honey, please go to your room. I'll bring you a little dinner, okay?" Iris said in her sweet voice.

Holy fucking shit. Was this really happening? Was I a goddamn prisoner?

"Char. You know I need your help," Dad pleaded, like he had so many times before. Only this time, something about it sounded different.

Or maybe I'd heard it differently.

"Please, Char. Please help me," he said with tears in his eyes.

I was such a sucker for his pain.

I wanted to run. And I wanted to help my father.

I couldn't do both.

32

BOWIE

"Bro, I'm seriously looking at a job at County."

Ace wore an expression of both resignation and defiance. It was one of the things I liked best about him, that he could balance life's contradictions. And I could appreciate his ambivalence. He had a big decision ahead of him. But he was a smart guy who'd always land on his feet.

Our backgrounds weren't that dissimilar. Ace had grown up in a more hardscrabble environment than I had, and before he got it together, he did what every other kid around him was doing.

I'd been just a plain old fuck-up who didn't care

about anything until I had a science teacher who took an interest in me. That's when I began to change my tune.

But for Ace to be judged for the environment he was born in by that old dog Cole was bullshit. It stood against every reason that he and I became doctors in the first place—to help out people on the wrong side of opportunity.

I supposed it was why we'd become friends so quickly.

On the other hand, Flynn was from a family of doctors. He'd never wanted for anything. But he was as down to earth as they came, laughing at the elitism he'd grown up around, and creating a life that veered in the opposite direction. I had to admire that in a man.

The best part was how we all had similar tastes in women, and how our appetite for 'sharing' had worked out so well.

I had high hopes Char would accept our offer. But if she didn't, that would be fine. What was best for her was best for us all.

"You know," Ace continued, "if I have to leave, it won't be the worst thing. I will have done my time in the military, at a big private hospital, and then it will be time to move on to a public facility."

"Sounds like a good career to me, Ace."

One of the ER nurses stopped and waved at us before continuing on her way.

Ace laughed. "Jesus. Do they just throw their panties at you all day long?"

I lowered my voice. "Very fucking funny. Like the nurses don't do the same thing to you, especially the ones with a red head fetish."

I'd seen women in bars all over Ace because of his red hair. It was hilarious.

"So, what do you think Char will decide?" he asked.

Wish I knew.

I'd been thinking about that a lot. Probably too much. But it was so rare to find someone as awesome as Char, whom we all liked, too. Our working together was a bit out of our norm, but I was confident we'd figure it out if we were given the chance.

I was going to be optimistic. "She's an adventurous type of girl. I can see her joining us. But with her dad running Headlands, that could present some obstacles, especially given how douche-y the man is."

Ace shook his head. "I know, right? We meet a great woman, and her father is our boss's boss's boss. What the fuck."

Talk about a lousy break.

"What I find concerning is the great lengths she went to in order to hide it. Is she afraid of him? Or just plain embarrassed? Or both?" I said.

I'd supposed I'd be embarrassed if Biddle were my father. He was pretty much universally hated around the hospital and Char was acutely aware of that.

"And what about her and her sister being named after their father? How vain is that?" Ace added.

"Doctor Grier, you're needed in treatment room three," a nurse said, disappearing as fast as she'd appeared.

Ace and I popped to our feet.

"I'll let you go, man." He looked at his watch. "I have a case coming up, too."

As we walked past the nurses' station with Ace on his way to the elevator and me on my way to room three, Char's name was mentioned and caught our ear.

"Who didn't show up today?" a nurse asked.

"Char. Char Biddle. You know, that new floater. Rosso is so pissed she's ready to explode."

"Are you serious? She just full-on didn't show?" another one said.

"Yeah. But she'll get a pass. Anyone else would get a warning. But when your dad runs the place, I guess you can get away with murder."

Ace and I looked at each other. Char was not the kind of person to just not show up.

I lowered my voice and leaned closer to Ace. "I'm going to text her. I'll let you know what I find out."

"Keep me posted." He nodded and took off.

I couldn't butt into the nurses' conversation without raising suspicion, so I kept my questions to myself for the time being. But things did not feel right. Not at all.

As soon as I gave breathing exercises to a young

man who was not having a heart attack, but rather a panic attack over finding out his wife was pregnant, I sent Char a text.

is everything all right? why aren't you at work?

Nothing.

Char.

Still nothing.

What the fuck?

"No response at all," I said, settling into the lunch table with Ace and Flynn.

"I texted her too. Nothing," Flynn said.

I looked around the cafeteria. "Isn't she friends with one of the nurses? I think her name is Alice?"

I couldn't even think straight.

"This is bullshit. We should not have to be sitting here in the dark," Ace said. "Let's just find out where her dad lives and head over there."

I took a deep breath. "I don't think she would want that, which is probably why she kept her living arrangements from us for so long. The last thing she wants is for her dad to know she's involved with us."

Flynn nodded. "Okay. Then one of us needs to talk to Rosso. Who's the best at sucking up to a pain in the ass?" he asked, shaking his head.

They both looked my way.

"Bowie, she tells people she used to be 'involved' with you," Ace said, rolling his eyes.

The woman was crazy. But I kept her under control by being as nice as possible. You never knew which way she was going to turn.

And if she were envious of Char, as she was of many of the young, attractive nurses, getting information out of her wasn't going to be easy.

CHAR

I wasn't a prisoner.

And yet I still couldn't walk out the door.

What the fuck was wrong with me? I was paralyzed by some bizarrely powerful loyalty toward my father—a man who didn't see me as much more than an asset to trade to get what he really wanted.

Every time I fantasized about telling him to fuck off, I saw the broken man he'd turned into when my mom had hit the road—someone who couldn't eat, sleep, or take care of his young daughters.

It had broken my heart. For some reason it still did.

"Char? Can you come down to the library to talk? Please?" he asked through my bedroom door.

I'd been holed up there since the night before, when I'd watched Alice's taillights fade into the night.

She'd texted me immediately.

what the fuck is going on? do I need to call the police?

I'd thought of the police as well. But I'd ruled them out. It wouldn't change anything. It wasn't like Dad and Iris were holding me in their house at gunpoint. If push came to shove, I could certainly walk out their door.

But I didn't.

I hated that Alice was worrying about me.

i'm ok. sorry to make you worry. i'll fill you in tomorrow at work

But I didn't *go* to work.

When I got up after a mostly sleepless night, Dad told me he'd called the hospital and let them know I needed a sick day. He said not to worry. To relax. Read a book. Watch a movie.

Yeah, I really felt like relaxing.

"Here I am," I said when I'd finally decided to join him. I tucked my legs under myself in one of his library's big leather club chairs and crossed my arms. I felt safer, coiled into a little ball.

"Char, when you left your cell phone in the kitchen, I saw text messages pop up from a couple of our doctors. I believe they were Bowie Grier and Ace Hardin?" He glared.

My stomach dropped, and I swallowed hard to ward off nausea.

"Oh, really?" I croaked, grateful Dad couldn't actually get *into* my phone to read the messages.

I'd not responded to the guys because one, I didn't know what to say and two, I was afraid they'd come over. That would do nothing but make a bad situation worse.

Think fast.

If Dad somehow found out about the guys, we'd be facing a disaster of nuclear proportion.

Fortunately, my brain, in survival mode thanks to the adrenaline making me want to puke, came up with something. It wasn't perfect. But it was something.

I tapped my temple like I'd just remembered. "Right. I'm working on a project with them. A study. They were probably wondering if I'd finished collecting the data they asked for."

Not bad for total bullshit.

His face relaxed. He'd bought it.

"Well, that's nice you're contributing to the work of the hospital. Not a lot of new nurses get opportunities like that. Of course, it probably helps that they know you're my daughter."

If he only knew.

I nodded. "Yeah. Good opportunity to get to know some people. Make a good impression."

Boy, I was good at this lying shit.

"I hope you've had some time to think about last night. It was why I didn't go to work today, and neither did you. We need to figure some things out. The

Quinns were not happy when they left last night. Not at all."

I had a feeling he was going to get to this.

"Well, Dad—" I started to say.

But he cut me off. Because of course.

He put his hand up like a *stop* sign, since anything I had to say to him was secondary to his thoughts. "You'll go back to work tomorrow, explain you had a family emergency, and no one will ask a thing. After work, Billy will pick you up and you will apologize to him. I've arranged everything with his father."

Did Billy just do everything his father told him to? What an imbecile.

'Course I supposed I wasn't much better.

"Dad, I really don't want—"

"Char," he said, interrupting me again, wearing what Franny and I used to call his 'sad face.' "I need your help with this. I am desperate. Your stepmother and I are desperate."

Was he actually begging me?

"Please, Char."

My head was whiplashing between the offensiveness of his request, and some sort of familial loyalty.

But after the shitshow of the night before, I knew if I wanted to get away from him, I had to move carefully.

Maybe even play along a little.

I forced a small smile. "Sure, Dad. I'll help you. I'm not crazy about Billy, but for you I can… figure it out."

He leaned back in his chair, victory written all over his face. "I knew I could count on you just like I could count on your sister Franny. She wasn't wild about marrying Scott, but she's made the best of it, and look at them now. With their new baby, they're a happy little family."

I'm pretty sure Franny was on high doses of antidepressants.

Dad was also oblivious to the fact that Franny hadn't really cared who she married as long as he had money and made babies with her.

You'd think he might grasp the differences between the two of us. But I guess people like him don't see what they don't want to see.

"Dad, why did Mom leave?"

His eyes widened in surprise. We'd never talked about her much.

"You know very well she left because she didn't want to be part of our family. That she didn't love any of us."

The familiar stab of that story struck me in the gut like it always had, which was why I supposed it didn't come up more. But for some reason I no longer believed it was the whole truth.

"She left so long ago. Why are you even thinking about her?" he asked.

I wasn't sure. But it might have something to do with seeing my dad's true colors, and wondering if she'd seen the same so many years ago.

34

CHAR

"Hi, Billy," I said, climbing into his glossy Corvette.

I didn't know that anyone under the age of fifty drove a Corvette.

He glared at me and put the car in gear as soon as I'd closed my door. Didn't even wait for me to put my seatbelt on.

He stared straight ahead as he navigated rush hour traffic until we arrived at one of the more popular restaurants in town. Two high-school age valets opened each of our car doors.

"Park it away from anybody else. I don't want any scratches," he barked.

I kept my head down as I followed the maître d' to our table. It wasn't like I knew a ton of people, but I sure didn't want anyone seeing me with Billy. My time suffering through his company was going to come to an end soon, one way or the other. God forbid anyone should think we were an item.

Once seated, he still didn't look at or speak to me.

Oh, glorious punishment. Maybe we could go through the whole meal without speaking? The fool had no idea how grateful I was for his juvenile cold shoulder treatment.

He finally set his menu aside and looked at me with a tilted head and pursed lips.

Holy shit. Was he going to scold me? I bit my lip to keep from laughing.

"Do you have anything to say to me, Char?" he snapped.

Yup. He was.

I wanted so badly to fuck with him, but I knew I had to play along, at least for a little while.

"I'm sorry, Billy, for last night," I said with all the fake regret I could muster.

He looked at me suspiciously. Maybe he wasn't so dumb.

To reinforce my point, I held my wine glass up. I knew I should have done something like take his hand, but I just couldn't bring myself to touch him. "Truce?"

He sniffed. "Yeah. I suppose."

The next half hour crept by. It was agony. Billy

talked at me the entire time, except for when he was shoveling food in his mouth, never leaving a moment for me to join the conversation or asking me a thing about myself.

Piece of shit.

Halfway through dinner, I caught a movement in my peripheral vision. And it wasn't the waiter.

"Char. Hello."

I looked up and choked a little on my halibut. This could be a problem.

Fuck if it wasn't Bowie.

And Flynn.

And Ace.

After clearing my windpipe, my mouth opened and closed. But no sound came out.

"Here, honey, drink some water," Billy said, eyeing the three guys suspiciously.

"Um, you okay, Char?" Ace asked.

I took a shaky breath. "Hello. Yeah, I'm good. My fish went down the wrong way. You know how that is." I belted out a laugh that sounded as fake as it actually was.

"We missed you at work today," Bowie said.

Right. That work thing…

I nodded frantically. "Yeah. Had a family emergency."

He wrinkled his brow while Billy looked between the two of us, scowling.

"But I heard you just didn't show up."

Huh?

"Oh, my father called my boss for me," I said.

How was I going to get out of this situation? And what were the fucking chances of running into these guys, here, on this night?

Think, girl.

Bowie frowned. "Are you sure? That he called? It doesn't sound like he did. People were wondering where you were. Some people even texted you."

Yup, I'd gotten those texts.

And it looked like Dad lied about notifying the hospital for me. What a guy.

Billy, tired of being ignored, extended his hand. "I'm Billy Quinn. Char's fiancé."

Oh no.

Bowie and Flynn paled but remained otherwise stone-faced. Ace was a little more reactive, scraping his hand through his hair and wrinkling his face in surprise.

I jumped in, as if there were something to say about the situation that would make sense of it.

"Oh, Billy, I don't know that I'd say that. But I'd like you to meet some of the doctors I work with at Headlands."

The tension was excruciating as they sized each other up and cautiously shook hands.

"So, you're an ortho?" Billy said, more interested in Flynn than my having contradicted his claim to me.

Flynn nodded slowly.

"Cool," Billy said. "I have a pain in my knee," he started, flexing it and pointing to his problem.

"Char? What is up with this fiancé stuff?" Ace interrupted.

And there we had it.

"Why is it any of your business?" Billy snapped, forgetting about his knee.

It was time. Time to be done with the bullshit that was my life.

"Honey, are you okay?" Flynn asked, ignoring Billy, whose face was getting redder by the moment.

Actually, they were all ignoring Billy. Which was kind of delicious.

Their concern, and ability to see that something was seriously wrong, especially after the poisonous last twenty-four hours of my life, hit me just right.

Which is to say, elicited a flood of emotion I wasn't prepared for. Neither were any of the four men staring at me.

"I… you can't…" I got to my feet as my voice broke. I tried to blink away tears that were coming too fast to control.

Fuck. I didn't want to cry in front of any of these guys.

But Billy reached across the table and yanked me back down into my seat.

"Buddy. Why don't you take it easy?" Bowie said, peeling Billy's grip off me.

His head snapped back indignantly. "Excuse *me*," he said in a raised voice.

As if that would make the guys back away.

"This is my *fiancé*," he said in a louder voice.

But the guys were focused solely on me.

"Do you want to come with us?" Ace asked, extending a hand.

A sob exploded out of my mouth, and I nodded tearfully. I grabbed my purse and took his hand.

Billy jumped to his feet. "Who the hell do you think you are?" he screamed at Ace.

Heads were turning now.

I started to move toward the door with the guys, but stopped and turned around.

"Billy, did you really think I would ever marry you?"

His mouth fell open, and he threw his napkin on the floor. "Char. Sit back down. Now."

For a second, I felt sad for him.

"Goodbye, Billy."

"I'll tell you everything," I said, blowing my nose into the monogrammed hanky Flynn handed me. "I just need to catch my breath. And calm down."

Flynn reached across the front seat of his car as he steered us toward his place. "Take your time, sweetie. Everything will be fine now."

"Yeah, Char, wait till we get to Flynn's. We'll all have

a glass of wine, and you can fill us in on what the hell is going on," Bowie said.

I sighed. "Yeah. It will take a glass of wine or two to get through it all. Hey, what were you guys doing there in that restaurant, anyway?"

Flynn glanced over his shoulder to the backseat. "Ace, is it okay if we share your news?"

"Of course you can share it with Char. I mean, she's gonna tell us all her secrets, right? But let's wait for the wine."

I had to laugh at that. It *was* time. No more lies.

Not surprisingly, my phone was blowing up with texts from my father. Billy hadn't wasted any time getting his parents to do his bidding, and my dad hadn't wasted any time pressuring me to do his.

But there was one person I needed to be in touch with.

Alice.

hey. all is well. i'm with the guys. will call you later, I texted.

are you sure you're okay? she asked.

yeah. things are fine now. at last

35

FLYNN

We settled into my living room, which the guys called the 'clubhouse,' I suppose because we spent more time there than at anyone else's place.

And why not? My apartment, thanks to the largesse of my parents, was spacious and comfortable, and a great place to hang. The least I could do was share it with my buds.

And Char, of course.

Ace was pacing the room, ready to jump out of his skin while he was waiting for everyone to get comfortable with a glass of wine in their hands. Finally, he took a seat.

"Char. Who was that Billy guy? What the fuck is

going on?" he asked, literally sitting on the edge of his seat and tapping his foot.

She set her wine glass down, her eyes still red from the tears she'd tried so hard to hold in. There was a little smudge of black under her left eye, and her hair was mussed, falling out of the clip she'd used to secure it. The clingy pink dress she wore had wine spilled down the front of it from when Billy had grabbed her arm and she'd tried to pull free.

Thank god we'd come along when we had.

And in spite of her sad expression and slightly disheveled appearance, she was perfect. I couldn't take my eyes off her, and I'd be lying if I said I wasn't also thinking about taking that sexy dress off her...

But there'd be time for that later.

She took a deep breath. "My dad has wanted to open a clinic specializing in radiology services as a business venture. He's been trying to raise money for it for the past few years, and has apparently gotten pretty close. He just needs one more investor and he's good to go."

"Holy shit. That's a bold plan. But I know those places can be gold mines," Bowie said. "One of my med school friends is a radiologist and went to work for one. He gets part of the profits and all that shit."

Yup. My dad, who always had his eye out for a buck, wanted a piece of that action.

"I can imagine. That's what drew my dad to it. So

the last investor he's trying to get on board are his friends, the Quinns. Billy's parents."

Ah-ha. So that's where that little douchebag had come from. The one who'd tried to get me to look at his knee in a freaking restaurant.

Idiot.

"In order to get the Quinns' commitment, my dad and stepmom have been pressuring me to date their son, who apparently likes me. Billy's parents are in on it too, thinking that if he and I tie the knot, our families will be bound together and there will be no losing their investment should the business fail. Or something like that. I don't get the logic behind it all because it's all just so warped."

Ace threw his hands in the air. "What a bunch of fucking nutbags."

Ace could be rough around the edges, but I liked how he got right to the point.

Char buried her face in her hands as her voice broke. "But he's so horrible. Total douchebag asshole. So full of himself. He disgusts me."

We guys looked at each other. What a wild goddamn story.

She raised her head and looked at each of us. "That's not even the best part."

I was afraid to ask what was.

"Okay. Try us," Bowie said.

"The other night… he proposed."

Silence filled the room while Char sipped her wine.

The only sound was the clink of her glass on the coffee table.

But Ace sprang up again, raising his hands like a *stop* sign. "Wait, wait, wait. Proposed? Like *marriage* proposed?"

Char nodded, wrinkling her face like she'd smelled something bad. "Can you believe it? Right in front of his parents and mine. What was really fucked up was that they all thought I'd jump at the chance. But I freaked. I ran to my room and locked the door."

I wished she'd called one of us. And now I knew her father was an even bigger jerk than the hospital scuttlebutt had let on. He was downright diabolical.

"Okay. So, why wasn't that the end of it?" Bowie asked.

Char pressed her lips together. "Well, it should have been. But my dad can be very persuasive. Basically he begged me, saying that I held the key to his success. All I had to do was let Billy in my life. If I did, the Quinns' money, and the successful business he was dreaming of, would all be his."

"He put all that on *you*?" Ace growled, his voice getting louder with each word.

Her face was washed with despair. "You see, ever since our mom left, my sister and I pretty much did anything we could to make him happy. He was so destroyed by it all, and we were just kids. It was like we had to help him take care of us. Otherwise, we didn't know what would happen to us."

Bowie let out a huge rush of air and let his head drop, blown away like we all were, by Char's incredible story.

"So, he and your stepmom have basically been manipulating the shit out of you?" Ace asked.

She nodded slowly. "Yeah. I guess I let them. I'll take responsibility for that. My sister let them, too. But I'm done. He doesn't give a damn about me."

Mind blown.

My own parents were pains in my ass, but at least they wanted what they thought was best for me. They didn't look at me as an expendable business venture. How could someone do that to another person, much less their daughter? I'd seen how hard Char worked, and how compassionate she was with her patients. She deserved better.

And I was going to make sure she got it.

She let out a long breath. "Wow. It feels good to have that off my chest. Now I'm hungry," she laughed.

I pulled up the local Chinese take-out menu on my phone so we could all order.

While Char made her selection, I had questions. "Who are your father's other investors?"

"I'm not really sure, but I think some of them are from the hospital's board of directors. He's friendly with several of them, especially the wealthy ones. Now I know why."

Hmmm. I made a mental note to call my father first thing the next morning. While it was only nine p.m., if

I called my parents at this hour, they'd be alarmed. I needed the conversation with my dad to be casual. Offhand.

Char leaned back on my sofa. "Thank you so much for listening. And saving me tonight. I never thought my evening would end up here. I'm so glad it did."

Bowie, seated next to her, took her hand, and raised it to his lips, kissing her palm and forearm, all the way up to her elbow.

Her expression transformed from one of unhappiness and worry to relaxation. And sexiness.

Ace, done pacing, helped himself to a seat on the other side of her, where he kissed her neck.

A small moan escaped her lips.

Our girl had been to hell and back. We were going to make her forget it all, if only for a short time.

While the guys were working on either side of her, Char looked up at me with those beautiful eyes, no longer red from crying, but bright with relief at having made some difficult decisions.

And I liked to think from our support, as well.

"Baby, that's fucking sexy, seeing Ace and Bowie work you over," I said, dying to stroke my growing cock.

But there'd be time for that.

"Yeah?" she said with a coyness that almost made me explode in my pants. "Guys, I think Flynn likes watching."

I nodded at her. "We all like watching, baby."

She stood and walked toward me, leaving Ace and Bowie on the sofa smiling and anticipating a show. As she moved, she untied her dress at the waist, and it swung open, revealing a low-cut bra and thong panties. She shimmied out of the dress and stood before us all, bold and sexy as hell.

I pulled one of her tits out of her bra, rubbing my palm over its sharp point, and reached between her legs, astonished by the heat radiating through her panties. I slid the fabric aside, and dove between her puffy lips to find her soaked with excitement. I paused one finger at her opening, and when I pushed inside an inch, she gasped, her walls contracting and begging for more.

Pulling my fingers back out, I pushed one in her mouth.

"I want you to know how you taste."

"Mmmm," she said, her beautiful lips closing around my finger.

"Now turn around."

She rotated until her back was to me and she faced the guys.

"Close your eyes, please," I whispered.

I unhooked her bra, which fell to the floor, and slipped her panties down so she could step out of them. I ran my hands over her shoulders to her tits, closing my fingers on her nipples until she gasped, reflexively trying to move away from me.

But my arms were around her. She was going nowhere.

Ace and Bowie wore serious, intent expressions as they watched me work Char over. When Bowie gestured toward her bare sex, I reached over her heated skin, back to her soaked folds where I'd been moments before. I continued kneading her breast with my one hand, alternately stroking and pulling her nipple, and used my other hand to open her pussy lips for the guys to see.

"Fuck dude," Bowie said, squirming in his seat. "That's what I'm talking about."

"You like it, baby?" Ace asked. "You like how Flynn is showing us your pretty pussy?"

She nodded, mumbling something affirmative.

My girl was turned on as hell.

Grinding my cock against her ass, I put a hand under her chin and turned her in my direction. "You want me to fuck you, baby?" I said into her ear.

"Yeah, Flynn," she said breathlessly. "Will you fuck me?"

"I will. And do you want Ace and Bowie to take out their dicks for you?"

Without a word, her head bobbed up and down again.

The guys didn't need any more prompting than that.

"Okay, baby, I'm gonna walk you toward the guys."

When she was a couple feet from them, I bent her at

the waist into a ninety-degree angle, and she leaned onto the guys sitting before her.

"Move your feet apart," I said, grabbing a condom from my pocket and dropping my pants.

When I'd sheathed myself and Char's ass was in the air, I opened her pussy to make way for my cock.

"Fuck, baby, you're so juicy. Are you ready for me?"

Kissing Ace, all she could do was nod and wiggle her ass in my direction. I slipped my cock inside, and she screamed with pleasure.

She held onto Ace and Bowie for leverage, and pushed back against me like a bucking animal, her pussy begging for me.

Holy fuck. I squeezed my eyes shut to hold my orgasm, hoping to wait at least until Char was moaning with her own. It didn't take long.

"Oh god, I'm coming," she cried.

The moment was explosive, with Char coming on my cock, and Ace and Bowie stroking their own dicks right in her face.

I slammed her pussy one last time and an explosion worked its way from my balls to my cock head. I held myself deep inside while I released my load. When I finally pulled out, she fell into the arms of the guys.

Goddamn, she was amazing.

36

FLYNN

"It's very nice to see you, Dr. Morrow. Please, make yourself at home. Can we get you any coffee?" Charles Biddle asked, nodding at his admin.

Yeah, I was in the office of the CEO of the fucking hospital.

I waved my hand. "Please, call me Flynn. Dr. Morrow is my father. And no coffee, thank you."

The door to Biddle's sumptuous office closed, and it was just the two of us.

I wondered if board members knew he had such nice digs. Then I remembered Char had said he was friendly with several of them. With the right relationships, you could get approval for just about anything.

The only photos around were of himself and board members. No photos of his daughters or second wife.

Biddle sat back in his seat. I could see a slight resemblance between him and Char, and it was clear he was probably once a handsome young man. But his eyes lacked the warmth that hers held, such that it was difficult to look at him for too long without needing a break.

"Tell me, Flynn, how is your father now that he's retired? We worked together for so many years. I really do have to call him for lunch."

Biddle had been part of the hospital administration while my dad was on staff. But my dad had never liked him.

The ironic thing was that Biddle had no freaking idea.

"My dad is well. Enjoying retirement. So, I'll get straight to the point, Mr. Biddle—"

He held his hands up. "Please, Flynn, call me Charles."

I smiled at his invitation. "Sure. Charles, my father and I heard you're looking for investors for a radiology clinic."

Biddle straightened up in his seat, and his face brightened, like a dog who knows he's about to be fed.

"We are looking for a good investment," I continued. "We think you could be a good bet, and we'd like to know more."

Beaming, Biddle looked like he'd won the lottery.

In a way, I guessed he had.

He clapped his hands together. "That's great news, Flynn. I don't know why I didn't think to come to you and your father to begin with. You would be wonderful business partners, just incredible additions to the team. In fact..."

He paused, studying me as he tapped his fingers on his desk.

"...there is a vacancy on the board of directors. I wonder if your father would be interested."

Um, no. The last thing my dad would want was to be associated with Charles Biddle.

"Well, how about that," I said, feigning excitement. "He'd probably be thrilled at the opportunity."

Just then, Biddle's door flew open.

"Charles, we have to get this shit straightened out ASAP—"

Biddle waved his hand and the visitor stopped short as soon as he spotted me. His eyes grew wide, and he looked from Biddle to me and back.

"Goodness," he said with sudden formality, "I'm so sorry. Didn't know you were in a meeting, Charles."

Biddle beckoned him over. "Hold on. I want you to meet Les Morrow's son, Flynn. You remember Les, don't you? Retired a couple years ago? Flynn here followed in the old man's footsteps and went into ortho. Flynn, this is our CFO, Tom Prior. He handles all things related to money here at Headlands."

I stood to shake the man's hand. I'd seen him in the

hallways and the cafeteria once or twice, but the administration and the medical staff seldom mixed.

He smiled nervously. "Well, it's great to meet you. Give my regards to your dad, please."

And he was gone as quickly as he'd arrived.

I glanced at my watch. "I need to run, Charles. I have rounds in a bit. But let's talk further about the clinic."

He popped to his feet. "Flynn, I like to move fast on finalizing business relationships. Shall I have my attorney draw up the papers?"

Jesus, he really was desperate for money.

"Sure," I said, not wanting to give myself away. "I'll talk to my father about next steps."

"Great Flynn. So glad you came by. I think when you look over the clinic prospectus, you'll be very impressed with the numbers. I figured we'll be profitable in less than two years' time."

"Sounds exciting, Charles."

We shook hands and I was out of there, my fact-finding mission a success.

One my way back to ortho, I dialed Char, hoping like hell she'd pick up.

37

CHAR

"You've been written up. Consider this a warning."

I looked at Rosso, where she sat behind her desk in her tiny office, arms crossed, looking very satisfied with herself.

How does someone take joy in giving out a warning?

"Giovanna—"

"It's *Nurse Rosso*."

Ugh.

"Yes. Nurse Rosso, I had a family emergency, and my dad assured me he let you know I'd be out for the day."

She bristled at the mention of my dad.

"He most certainly did not call in for you. Char, you cannot count on your dad's position here to help you coast through your responsibilities here."

Wait. What?

"Nurse Rosso, are you saying you never got a call or some other sort of message from my father? He assured me he let you know."

The way she looked at me, like I was full of shit, answered my question.

That fucker. As if he weren't already causing enough harm, he got me in trouble at work. The question was, why? Didn't he know any failings on my part could reflect on him, just like his would on me?

Or was it just to remind me of the power he had over me? Rather, the power he *used to have* over me?

"Nurse Rosso, I am so sorry. My father was to call in my absence."

It wasn't bad enough that Dad had screwed me over, but now the other nurses in my group were probably pissed at me. Being short a nurse was a hardship on everyone.

And Rosso was taking great pleasure in doling out her sentence.

I never should have trusted him. He set me up.

I didn't blame her for being pissed. So, I decided to eat crow to get back in her good graces.

"I had no idea. I feel awful. I understand your

writing me up. Under the circumstances, I completely deserve it." I stood to go.

Her expression softened. She'd been clearly ready for a fight, but I needed to save my energy for other things.

"You don't want to get another warning, Char," she added as a parting shot, just to make sure I knew she was boss.

"You're right. I apologize for burdening the team."

She gave me a satisfied smile, and turned back to her computer.

I exited Rosso's office and hustled into the stairwell so she couldn't see where I was going. I needed to keep her out of my business.

"Hi there," I said to my dad's admin once I'd reached the top floor. I extended my hand. "You must be new."

They were always new. My dad couldn't keep an admin to save his life.

She looked me up and down, then took my hand with her fingers, delivering one of the worst hand-shakes I'd ever gotten.

"I'm Char Biddle."

She squinted to look at my ID badge, and then real-ization washed over her face.

Yeah. I was *that* Char Biddle.

"Oh, I'm sorry, honey. I didn't know you were Charles's daughter. I'm Eleanor. Your dad's out at a meeting. Expected back in… twenty minutes."

I smiled sweetly. It was hard to resist a kind nurse.

"I'll just wait in his office then," I said, opening his office door.

"Oh, Char, I don't think he'd want—"

But I pulled it shut before she could finish.

Chances were low she'd kick me out since I was the boss's daughter. I pressed my ear against his door and heard her desk phone ring. A phone call might buy me a couple minutes. But I twisted the office door's lock just in case. Of course, she had a key she could use if she really wanted—I just needed to slow her down if she decided she wanted to watch over me.

And if she asked why I'd locked the door? I'd tell her it was a simple accident.

So much for quitting lying.

I zipped over to my dad's desk and began rifling through the tidy stack of papers that had most likely been arranged by Eleanor. In one pile, there was a pad with handwritten notes on it, which included Flynn's name, as well as what looked like the names of a couple banks I'd never heard of.

Interesting.

Below the pad were invoices. I had no idea what hospitals spent with their suppliers, but from the look of it, they spent a lot. The smallest invoice was for ten thousand dollars. The largest was for four hundred thousand dollars.

Jesus. I knew running a hospital wasn't cheap, but I didn't realize it involved expenses like that.

I grabbed my phone and snapped photos of it all. I

had no idea whether any of it would be useful, but I had a feeling I'd know soon. Just as I dropped my phone into my pocket and I pushed my dad's desk chair in, I spotted a single pearl earring on the carpet next to his garbage bin.

I crouched to get a closer look. It didn't look like anything Iris would wear—she preferred flashy jewelry since her pretentiousness rivaled my dad's. I picked up the small stud, turning it over in my fingers. Its back was missing, and it was real gold.

An earring on the floor of my dad's office. What the hell?

Maybe it was Eleanor's. Or someone from the cleaning staff. Or it simply belonged to one of the many people who helped run the hospital. But why was it right next to Dad's desk?

I dropped the earring where I'd found it and hustled to get the hell out of there.

"Thanks Eleanor, I'll catch up with my dad later. I need to get back to work."

She smiled and gave me a little wave.

"Nice meeting you, sweetie," she chirped.

38

CHAR

Even though I was busy as hell with patients, running from one to the next carrying out various doctors' orders, the day dragged because I hadn't seen any of the guys once, not even in the cafeteria, which I'd had five minutes to run to for a yogurt.

I had run into Alice, though, even though we were assigned different departments.

"What the fuck, girl?" she asked, dragging me into the ladies' room. She looked under all the stall doors to make sure we were alone.

"You won't believe the shit going on in my life right now."

She put her hands on her hips. "No kidding. What

was that all about when they wouldn't let you out of the house? I thought I'd have to storm the place."

"I'm sorry, Alice. I should have just left, but my dad begged me to stay and help him. He keeps trying to push me into dating that loser Billy Quinn. Dad is trying to get the Quinns to invest in his new business venture."

I couldn't bring myself to tell her about the ridiculous marriage proposal that had ignited the night's shitshow. I was still processing the bizarreness of it.

"Okay. That is messed up. Your dad can't tell you who to date."

She was right.

And yet…

"It's complicated, Alice, but ever since my mom left, Franny and I have done just about anything he wanted to make him happy. We felt so sorry for him. It's bullshit, I know. Talk about family dysfunction."

"That is bullshit," she said, frowning. "In every other area of your life you are confident and assertive. But you let your dad push you around. I don't get it."

I didn't get it either. But I was starting to.

"Look, Alice, I have to get back to work. Rosso was all over my ass this morning. But hey, I'll see you at your place later. Thank you so much for letting me crash there. You are a seriously amazing friend."

I threw my arms around her for a quick hug, and got back to my floor before Rosso found a reason to write me up for something else.

Without even changing into my street clothes, the moment I was off work I ran to my car, which I'd just wrestled out of the repair shop where it had languished for a month.

Not surprisingly, my car had been ready to be picked up for weeks. My dad had told the mechanic I was out of the country and to store the vehicle for him.

Yup, I'd fallen prey to my dad's efforts to control me once again. But now wasn't the time to dwell on that.

I sped over to Dad's house in order to get in and out before he got home from work, or Iris returned from one of her charity meetings.

I parked my car in the driveway on the side of the house so no one would see it, and sneaked in through the kitchen. Before Dad and Iris had gone broke, there'd be any number of household staff cooking or cleaning. Now, the house was dead quiet.

I headed straight for the library, off of which was my dad's cozy home office. I rifled through the stacks of papers on his desk and found some banking documents.

The banks he'd had listed on his notepad at work?

These were from those very banks.

I scrolled through the photos on my phone to confirm it, then photographed these new findings, as well.

Now I knew why I hadn't recognized any of them. They all had addresses in the Cayman Islands.

What the hell? Why would Dad have bank accounts in the Cayman Islands?

I was just finishing snapping my pictures when Iris burst into the room.

"Char, honey, what are you doing in here?"

My heart thumped against my chest, and I pretended to scroll through my phone. "Iris. Hi. I was um, looking for some of that info on weddings Dad had told me about."

Her face exploded in happiness.

"Oh, let me find that for you," she said, flipping over the bank papers and rifling through another stack. "I'm so excited to help you plan your wedding. That is, *if* you accept Billy's proposal." She nudged me, giggling.

So. Fucking. Clueless.

"Yeah. I have a lot to think about, don't I? Hey, do you think my mother should be invited?"

To say horror washed over her face would be an understatement. "Uh, wh… why would you do that?" she stammered with a nervous laugh.

I shrugged, hoping that playing dumb would get more information out of her. "I don't know. Just a crazy idea, I guess."

Her lips drew into a thin line that not even all her facial fillers could disguise.

I tilted my head. "Iris, do you know much about her?"

Her eyes widened. "Nope. No, I don't. Only that she took off on your dad and you girls. It was a terrible, terrible thing," she said, shaking her head.

Yeah. Iris was a lousy liar. There was more to the story than either my dad or she were letting on.

It was high time I woke the fuck up and started asking some of the questions I'd been afraid to all my life. I might get some answers I didn't like, but I could deal with that.

None of the other shit I'd been confronted with had killed me yet.

39

ACE

"You won't freaking believe this."

Bowie and I watched Flynn pace the floor of his living room two days after he'd bullshitted Biddle about investing in his business.

"What won't we believe?" Bowie asked. "Did you hear from your friend at the DA's office?"

"I sure as hell did. He let me know Charles Biddle has been under investigation by them for some time. He couldn't share any details, but he must have done something big to have drawn their attention."

Holy shit. What the hell had we stumbled on?

"Does Char know?" I asked.

"I don't think so, Ace. I just found out a few minutes ago from my buddy over there."

"Did you share with him the stuff Char found? That she took pictures of?" Bowie asked.

I nodded. "Yeah. I sent it all over to him. Biddle's up to something with offshore accounts, that much is clear. I mean, it could all be legit. Plenty of people have offshore accounts. But he doesn't really have the level of assets that your average person like that does."

Yeah. Something wasn't adding up. I wouldn't normally wish bad things on anyone, but since we'd learned how horrible he'd been toward Char, all bets were off. If there was anything we could do to bring that man down, we were going for it.

Even though it didn't look like the relationship we'd hoped for with Char was going to materialize.

She'd stopped by the night before on her way to her friend Alice's house. She was done living with her father and stepmother, thank god.

She'd shared with us what she'd found on his desks both at the hospital and at home, forwarding the photos to our phones. "I don't really know what this means, but someone else might be able to connect the dots. My dad is nearly broke. He's in debt up to his eyeballs, so I don't really know what he'd be doing depositing money overseas."

I didn't either, but I had a feeling it wasn't anything on the up and up.

"Another thing I wanted to discuss with you guys…" she started.

Everyone's ears perked up.

I'd be lying if I didn't admit my pulse sped up. If she was getting at what I hoped she was, there was a lot at stake for all of us.

She looked from one of us to the other with the adorable, crooked smile that kept her lovely face from looking Barbie Doll perfect.

"You guys have been good to me. I'm so appreciative. And look at all you're doing now to help me. I don't know how I will ever repay you."

I could think of a few ways…

"What are you getting at, Char?" Bowie asked.

She looked down at her hands, avoiding us. "I'm sorry, but can't be with you. I feel like someone would get hurt, and I couldn't live with myself if that happened. It kills me to say this…" Her voice broke, and she finally looked up, her face laced with sadness.

A pit of disappointment landed in my stomach. Serious disappointment. A quick glance at Bowie and Flynn told me I wasn't alone.

I took a deep breath. "It's okay, sweetie. We'll always be here for you, regardless."

She nodded and sniffed. "Thank you, Ace. That means… so much."

I was bummed. I couldn't deny it. But if it wasn't right for her, it wasn't right for any of us. It took a lot of trust to do what we guys did, and it didn't work for most people. We knew that. We'd invited her to be part of our lives. She declined our offer, and I respected that.

She said goodnight, and headed over to Alice's.

And we guys sat there for a long time.

I was at the hospital, getting ready to see a patient, when I got a text from Flynn.

biddle has been fired

Holy fucking shit.

meet me in the ER on-call room

I got someone else to see my patient and ran downstairs, where I found Flynn and Bowie.

We closed the door to the room, fortunate to have found it empty.

"What's going on?" Bowie asked. "How did you find out?"

Flynn lowered his voice even though we had the room to ourselves. "My father just called me. He knows people on the board of directors."

Bowie let out a low whistle.

Jesus.

He continued. "Apparently, he'd been pressuring board members to invest in the radiology business he's trying to build. They'd had enough and fired his ass."

Whoa.

"So what is the DA working on?" Bowie asked. "Same thing or something different?"

Flynn shrugged. "Your guess is as good as mine, given the paperwork Char dug up. But this is certainly not Biddle's day."

No shit.

All I could think of was finding Char to let her know what was going on before she was blindsided by the news.

"Guys, where's Char today?" I asked.

"Here. In the ER," Bowie said.

I headed for the door. "C'mon. We have to find her."

Our beautiful girl was at the nurses' station, making notes in a patient's record, when who should come bounding out of the elevator but her father.

He did not look happy.

"Char," he yelled across the room.

Her eyes widened, and she slowly turned. Actually, everyone turned.

"C'mon. We're going home," he barked.

She frowned, but when she caught sight of us, I could swear she stood a little taller. I could have been flattering myself, but I'd like to think we gave her a boost of courage.

"No," she said simply.

He crossed the room with amazing speed, and slapped her across the face with an open palm.

Char stumbled and screamed, as did several of the

other nurses. Her hand flew to her face and her coworkers ran to help.

By the time I turned back to Biddle, Flynn had already tackled him to the floor.

"Get your fucking hands off me, Morrow. I know your father, and he's not going to be happy about this."

I was pretty sure he was wrong about that.

In seconds, security was on the scene, and they dragged him outside while waiting for the police to arrive.

We all turned our attention back to Char, who was crying in the arms of another nurse.

Bowie elbowed his way in. "Let me look at her, please," he said, turning her neck and feeling her jaw.

While he did that, the ER got back to business as usual. Fortunately, none of the patients had witnessed the outburst. Nurse Rosso, however, had watched the whole thing from a distance and was now motoring to get out of there as fast as she could, looking back over her shoulder before disappearing into an elevator.

Strange. Why didn't she try to help? She was Char's boss, after all.

"C'mon. Let's move to a treatment room," Bowie said, supporting Char with an arm around her shoulders.

As soon as we had privacy, I realized she was shaking. I grabbed a blanket and wrapped it around her.

"Thank you, Ace. I... I'm so humiliated," she said, her teeth chattering.

Fuck. Poor thing was in shock.

"I'm quitting," she mumbled. "I can't work here anymore."

"Take a deep breath, sweetie. You don't have to decide anything right now," Bowie said, rubbing his hand on her back.

"Char, you know your dad got fired just before he came down to the ER, right?"

She nodded. "One of the other nurses had just told me. And I wasn't surprised at all to see him in the ER. If he couldn't work for Headlands, he didn't want me to either. Didn't think he was going to haul off and hit me, though," she said with a sad laugh, rubbing her red cheek.

I poked my head out the ER door just in time to see Biddle loaded into the back of a cop car.

"Looks like this isn't your dad's day," I said.

"He's had this coming for a long time. It might not be his day, but it sure is mine."

40

CHAR

"Iris?" I said when she'd picked up on the first ring.

"Hi, sweetie."

I almost felt sorry for her. Almost.

I took a seat in Bowie's office and he left, closing the door behind himself to give me some privacy. The guys had been so kind, defending and protecting me.

My guys.

Oh shit. Did I really just say that?

"Hey, Iris, some things happened at Headlands today that I need to tell you about."

"Oh. Is everything okay?"

I could imagine her swanning around the house in

one of her Escada suits. She dressed to the nines even on days when she had nowhere to go.

It had always blown her mind when I hung out in yoga pants and a sweatshirt. She said you never knew *who might stop by.*

She was right. You never knew. But no one ever just *stopped by* our house.

"No, Iris, everything is not okay. Dad just got fired. And then he hit me in front of everyone, and is now in police custody."

In the background, I heard something clatter to the floor.

"Oh my god. Oh my god," she said.

"Yeah. I just wanted to make sure you knew. It's terrible."

She stifled a sob. "I told him something like this would happen."

"I guess he just went too far with the board members, asking them to invest—"

Something else crashed. Was she throwing stuff?

She scoffed. "Is that what you think? Char, you have always been so naïve, just flitting through life, making T-shirts and following bands. You know how much that embarrassed your father?"

A tightening sensation settled in my throat, and my left temple throbbed. *Now* she was going to give me shit? She didn't have bigger things to worry about?

"What are you saying, Iris?"

"I knew it would catch up with him. I just knew it. You can only hide money for so long."

Hide money?

My dad had been hiding money?

"Iris, Dad was fired for pressuring the board members to invest in his radiology business. What money are you talking about? I thought he was broke."

She cackled. "Yeah, yeah. That's what you think, Char. How do you think he supported our lavish lifestyle?"

"How?" I asked in a small voice.

I figured Dad knew what he was doing. But I guess on some level I knew things weren't adding up.

And I hadn't wanted to upset him. He'd always been so sad…

"Did you know your father owns an airplane? A private jet?" she snapped.

What?

I was afraid to ask my next question, but I had to. "Wh… where did the money come from?"

There was silence for a moment.

"I can't tell you that."

"Well, what did you mean by *hiding money*?"

She huffed. "I… I didn't mean that."

"Does this have something to do with those banking documents from the Cayman Islands?"

"How do you know about those?"

"They were right on Dad's desk."

Something like a shriek nearly split my eardrums. "That fool! I knew he couldn't be trusted. He was always so careless and now look at him. Look at us. Look at me."

Her rant became hard to follow as she tore through the house.

"Iris, are you okay?"

"I'm done with that loser!" she screamed.

Things opened and slammed shut.

Packing, I supposed.

"I'm out of here. I've wanted a divorce from him for so long, and he always begged me to stick around. And you want to know something about your mother, Char?"

She knew more about my mom. I knew it.

"Yes, I do."

"He *drove* her away. *Paid* her to leave. If she hadn't, he would have had her committed and gotten custody of you girls, anyway."

"Wha… why?" I choked.

"He wanted a divorce so he could marry me, but she wouldn't agree. So he paid her off. Then he filled your head with lies about her not loving you. He even faked being depressed."

All those years…

"Why didn't he just let us go with her?"

"Because, Char, having children made him look good, especially when he took up with me. I was a nurse at the hospital."

Holy fuck. I'd known she was a nurse for a brief period, but not at Headlands.

"I knew your mom, Char. We were friends."

The drab wall I faced in Bowie's office took on a liquefied look, and bright dots of different sizes bounced into my vision. I dropped the phone and leaned over the trash bin just in time to get sick.

41

CHAR

I woke up on the sofa at Flynn's. I knew the guys had walked me out of the hospital and helped me into his car, but the memory was vague, like I'd dreamt it and I was trying to remember the details before it slipped away.

"Oh my god," I mumbled, touching the wet washcloth someone had placed on my head.

"Here. Take a sip of water," Ace said, propping me up.

I knew him by his red hair, but his face was a blur. I squeezed my eyes shut and took a sip. When I reopened them, things began to morph into view. I pushed myself up, and found Bowie and Flynn oppo-site me, sitting on the edges of their slick leather chairs.

I'd never been so happy to see them.

"Aren't you guys supposed to be at work?"

They looked at each other and laughed.

"I got someone to cover for me," Bowie said, looking to Ace.

"I was done with my shift."

We all turned to Flynn. "And I have to get back in" —he looked at his watch—"one hour. But you clearly needed to get out of the hospital, so we brought you here until you caught your breath."

I rubbed my hands over my face. "I'm still not sure I've caught my breath."

My phone buzzed in my pocket. It was Alice.

"Excuse me, guys," I said, holding up a finger.

"Jesus, Char. You okay?" she asked.

"Yeah. I'm with the guys. Can I call you later?"

"Yup," she said.

"So, there was more to the story than my dad pres-suring board members, according to my stepmother's rant," I said.

But the guys nodded. They already knew.

I shared the disjointed story Iris had spilled, still unsure of exactly what it meant. Flynn left the room to call his DA friend.

"So," Bowie started, looking at me, the crinkles around his eyes forming as a smile spread across his face, "now are you going to tell me what happened to your hand?"

Oh. That.

I rubbed the faint scar on my palm. It seemed so long ago that he'd stitched me up.

"My dad and Iris were fighting. She had a knife, and I tried to stop her."

He raised his eyebrows.

"I lied. Once again, to protect my father. And, I guess, myself."

"Old habits die hard," Ace said, putting an arm around my shoulder. "You've been through a lot, baby."

Flynn returned. "Holy shit. The DA was already on their way to take your dad in. And since he is now in custody for hitting you and causing a scene in the hospital, he saved them the trouble."

Glad I could help.

I rubbed the sore side of my face that he'd whacked with full force. I both hated him and was broken-hearted at the same time. But those days of feeling badly for him, and responsible for him, were disappearing in the rearview mirror. Fast.

Flynn returned to his seat, shaking his head. "Turns out your dad and his accomplices were taking real invoices from vendors and adding tens of thousands of dollars to their totals. Then, they would have the hospital pay the fake invoice with payment going directly to an offshore account rather than the vendor. The vendor invoice would then be paid out of *that*, and your dad and his cronies would keep what was left. They made a freaking fortune."

Thank god I was sitting because I thought I might pass out again.

That's how dad funded his lifestyle. That's how he bought a fucking *jet* airplane.

I just looked at my hands. I didn't know what to say. But the shame that passed over me was the worst thing I'd ever felt.

My own father. A criminal. A horrible, disgusting man. And what he'd done to my mother.

All these years I'd believed him.

Flynn continued. "As you can imagine, it would be impossible to run a scheme like this on your own. Several arrests are expected to be made, including the CFO guy I met when I was in your dad's office."

"I can't go back to Headlands," I said, shaking my head.

Bowie put his hands up. "Char, you have done nothing wrong. I understand the shame and humiliation, but that will pass. You've got to keep your head up high."

Ace and Flynn nodded in agreement.

My eyes filled with tears. What did I do to deserve the support of these amazing men? I'd turned down their offer of a relationship and yet, they still came to my rescue.

"You know, Char," Ace said, "I'm probably leaving to

go to County at the end of the year. Why don't you come with me?"

For the first time, it dawned on me that I was free to make whatever decisions I wanted.

Just as Bowie had suggested, I held my head up and went into work the next day. There were whispers and looks like I knew there would be—it was bound to happen. But I was fighting the shame I felt for the actions of my father. For some people, they were a reflection on me. But the only thing I'd done wrong was believe he was a good guy.

Boy had I been wrong. If he'd banished my mother when I was little, he'd undoubtedly been bad news long before then. And if he'd extorted my mother to stay away, did that mean I might be able to find her?

I knocked on Rosso's door, wanting to check in and, well, talk about everything that had been going on. I was sure she'd have something to say about the matter, but I wanted to assure her I was committed to the team. She didn't need to know I might want to hit the road at some point.

While I was knocking, one of the nurses from my orientation program happened by.

"Hey, Char." She gave me a big, friendly smile. I'd always liked her.

"Samantha, good to see you. Hey, I'm looking for Nurse Rosso. Have you seen her?" I asked.

Samantha's eyes widened. "Oh, I guess you haven't heard. She was… um…well, she's not with the hospital anymore. Something about being caught up in a scam involving kickbacks and falsifying invoices. Isn't that crazy?"

No. Fucking. Way.

She was working with my dad on his scam?

"Hey, gotta run, Char. Let's get coffee sometime and catch up, okay?"

"Sounds great, Samantha."

I tried the door to Rosso's office. It was unlocked, so I walked into the tiny, dark room she'd been so proud of. I felt around for the light switch, and when it flicked on, a series of ugly fluorescent lights sputtered on.

The place had been vacated in a hurry. There were some crumpled papers on Rosso's floor as if someone had missed the trash bin, and the pencil cup had been emptied out.

That would be just like her, to take every last pen and pencil with her.

In place of the nursing school diplomas she'd so proudly displayed were just empty hooks and the drawers of her metal desk were partially open. Her computer monitor and keyboard were still on the desk, but her laptop and docking station were missing, probably confiscated by the hospital IT department.

I sat in her chair, thinking what it was like to be her

—someone with little or no life, rumor had it, outside the hospital, and for whom being the boss of a bunch of junior nurses was everything.

Well, not everything. She wouldn't have gotten sucked into my dad's scheme if she were truly content with her lot.

I stood, getting ready to leave, when a little white dot on the tile floor caught my eye. I bent closer.

It was a tiny pearl earring in a gold setting.

42

CHAR

Change comes about in strange ways, I was learning. You think you're on one path, and the road veers. You follow the new one because it seems like there's no other choice.

But there's always a choice. And I'd made an important one.

I texted the guys to meet at Flynn's when everyone got off work that evening. I sneaked out a little early with Alice covering my shift, and went grocery shopping. A couple hours later when the guys arrived, Flynn's place was filled with the delicious scents of my cooking.

"Holy shit," Ace hollered, dropping his backpack in

the middle of the foyer, "what is cooking in that kitchen?"

He peeked around the corner and gave a low whistle.

I loved that he still flirted with me, considering the status of things.

Flynn and Bowie were right behind him.

"My place has never smelled so good, Char," Flynn said, lifting the lid off a pot and jumping out of the way of a billow of steam.

"Okay, guys. Out, out, out. But before you go, here." I'd lined up three wine glasses filled with a really good red I'd found in Flynn's collection. "Hope you don't mind I opened this, Flynn. It seemed like a good night to drink something special."

He tasted his and rolled his eyes. "This stuff is awesome. Seems like somebody knows her wine." He sidled up to me and smiled. I could tell he wanted to kiss me. Instead, I gave him a quick hug.

It was important to keep things uncomplicated. I didn't like complicated.

When dinner was ready, I called everyone to the table.

"Oh my god, this looks amazing," Bowie said.

I piled each plate with a juicy filet mignon, roasted vegetables, and an assortment of other side dishes.

When we sat down to eat, the place was finally quiet. For a few minutes, that was.

"Damn, where'd you learn to cook like this?" Ace asked.

"When my mom left, my sister and I had to learn how. Our dad was too depressed to take care of us. Or he was pretending to be depressed, that is."

Turned out Dad was quite the actor.

"Speaking of your mom, what are you going to do now that you know your dad chased her off? Do you think you can find her?" Flynn asked.

God, I hoped so. Over the last twenty-four hours of my life, she was pretty much all I had thought about. Reconnecting with her, if we *did* find each other, would not be easy. Dad had done a job on all of us.

But I needed to focus on the task at hand and went into the kitchen to return with dessert.

"What's that?" Ace asked, craning his neck to see.

I displayed my creation proudly. "An apple pie. And we have vanilla ice cream."

The room erupted in whistles and applause, and I cut into the steaming crust. I had to admit, I made a freaking killer apple pie.

I stood at the head of the table. "Okay, guys, before I serve, I have something to say."

I immediately had everyone's attention.

"I wanted to make dinner for you tonight to thank you for your support through this crazy-ass time."

"Our pleasure, Char," Flynn said.

"And I also have something very important to share with you."

They looked at me curiously.

"I wanted to tell you, if the offer still stands, that I'm on board with the crazy arrangement you proposed."

"Huh?"

"Did you just say—?"

"Could you repeat that please?"

I cleared my throat, still trying to process my decision, just like they were. "I mean to say that I want to be with you. All of you. I can't imagine my life any other way."

43

BOWIE

In the less-than-two-months since the Biddle scandal had been uncovered at Headlands Hospital, there had been a mass exodus of many of the staff, who, like me, had taken stock of their skills and how they were using them. Sometimes it takes a shakeup to remind you of who you were.

I was sad to leave Headlands. I couldn't lie. But the opportunity to head up the emergency department at County was just too good to pass up. Actually, it was the opportunity of a lifetime. Sure, there would be budget shortfalls and other challenges typical of that kind of facility, but the work would be rewarding on so many levels.

The best part was that I'd still see Char every day. She and her friend Alice had followed me to County after I'd followed Ace there. And rumor had it that Flynn would be joining us soon.

We'd hired Char to head up a program founded by Ace and me to get underprivileged kids interested in science. We met with science teachers at several middle schools and high schools and they helped us put together a plan consisting of classroom visits by doctors and nurses from every discipline and tours of the hospital for the kids. There were even opportunities for them to do some volunteering with us. It was a big hit already, and we were getting great publicity, which was good news for County.

I hoped I could do for some kid what someone did for me when I was floundering in school, unmotivated and lazy. I'd never forget the teacher who saw the potential in me and told me so.

I grabbed a quick shower before I left the hospital that night. We were meeting Char at her Dad's house where she was in the final stages of cleaning it out and prepping it for sale.

"Check this place out," Ace said when we'd arrived, doing a three-sixty to take it all in.

Biddle's had been a lavish house, fitting for a man of his ambitions. Too bad he never lived up to them.

"Guys, I finally made a decision about what to do with all this stuff," Char said, beaming. "Dad had put most everything in my name, I've been told by his attorney, so I'm auctioning it all, and the proceeds will benefit our new science program."

"Holy shit, that's awesome," Flynn said, picking up our girl and twirling her around. "But what are you going to do when the house sells?"

"I haven't decided yet," she said, looking from one of us to the other.

Flynn raised his hand. "You know *I* have a ton of room."

"Hey, hey, hey," Ace said. "I don't have the kind of room that Flynn does, but my apartment has views."

I rolled my eyes. "Okay. Hold on you two. Your places are nice. I'll grant you that. But I'm the one with a pool in my building."

Char giggled. "This is gonna be hard. I mean, guys, Bowie has a pool."

While we disputed who had the best living arrangement, Char sat back on a sheet-covered chair and just laughed at us.

After a minute we stopped and laughed with her.

Who knew where our girl would end up with so many awesome choices? But we did know she was ours, and we were hers, and that together we'd figure out any shit that came our way.

Just like we already were.

Did you like *Her Dirty Doctors*?

Learn more about the next book in the
Men at Work series,
Her Dirty Bodyguards

I hope you loved reading this book as much as I
loved writing it. Please visit my store to learn more
about my books, and to buy directly from me!
https://mikalaneshop.com/

ABOUT THE AUTHOR

Dear Reader:

I'm USA TODAY bestselling romance author Mika Lane, and am OBSESSED with bringing you sassy, steamy stories with imperfect heroines and the bad-a*s dudes they bring to their knees. I'll always bring you my signature humor and heat, topped off with a modern-day happily ever after.

My first book ever was *The Day I Ate the Milkyway*, a true fourth-grade masterpiece illustrated with crayons and bound with construction paper and glue. Nowadays, steamy romance gives purpose to my days and nights as I create worlds and characters that tickle the imagination. I live in magical Northern California with my own handsome alpha dude, sometimes known as Mr. Mika Lane, and two devilish cats named Chuck and Murray.

A dual citizen of the United States and Ireland, I have on more than one occasion spent my last dollar on a plane ticket somewhere, and am always planning my next escape. I often try new recipes on unsuspecting friends, search out hiding places to read undisturbed, and sadly kill every houseplant I bring home.

I LOVE to hear from readers when I'm not dreaming up naughty tales to share. Visit my online shop https://mikalaneshop.com/ and say hello https://mikalaneshop.com/pages/meet-mika.

xoxo, Mika